BOOKER & FITCH

DEATH
on
Opening
Night

LIZ HEDGECOCK   PAULA HARMON

WHITE
RHINO
BOOKS

Copyright © Liz Hedgecock, Paula Harmon, 2023

All rights reserved. Apart from any use permitted under UK copyright law, no part of this publication may be reproduced, stored in a retrieval system, or transmitted, in any form or by any means, electronic, mechanical, photocopying, recording or otherwise, without the prior written permission of the copyright owner.

This is a work of fiction. Names, characters, businesses, places, events and incidents are either the products of the author's imagination or used in a fictitious manner. Any resemblance to actual persons, living or dead, or actual events is purely coincidental.

ISBN-13: 979-8391991212

*To our children: Matt, Zoe, Otis and Felix,
despite whom we completed this book!*

CHAPTER 1

Fi Booker scanned the dining room in the Vine as she waited for Andy's return.

The Tudor pub was always warm and intimate, more so with the October night pressing against the windows. A fire crackled in the ancient hearth beneath a mantelpiece decorated with a mixture of evergreens, tiny pumpkins and orange fairy lights. Among the decorations were flyers for *Macbeth*, which would soon open at the Little Theatre. Someone had changed the daily specials board to read *Clamorous Harbingers*, *Cauldron Bubble*, and *Something Wicked* instead of Starters, Mains and Desserts. On the chimney breast, a carving of the Green Man was topped with a crown of plaited wheat and hawthorn berries.

Full of wine and good food, Fi imagined the pub as it might have been when it opened, twelve years before Shakespeare wrote *Macbeth*: rushes on the floor, tallow candles giving little light, men in rough clothes drinking ale from pottery cups and spooning stew from wooden bowls...

'Earth calling Fi!' Andy waved his hand in front of her eyes.

'Sorry! I was miles away.' Fi stood up. There was a brief tussle over her coat until she realised Andy was trying to help her into it. Chuckling, she let him do it, his fingers brushing her neck as he arranged the collar, his hand smoothing the back of the coat to settle it on her shoulders.

It was her second date with Andy, or rather the second since he'd asked if they could resurrect the fledgling relationship they'd abandoned the previous year. She'd agreed, thinking perhaps it could work now that she was less defensive, less secretive about her dreams. If the last few months had taught Fi anything, it was to be more open and trusting.

They'd had a lovely evening. Andy was attractive, with a tall, strong, slender figure, laughing blue eyes and dark hair flecked with a few distinguished silver strands. Being with him made Fi feel herself – not a widowed mum, a bookshop owner, or 'one of the women who dabbled in that murder', but simply Fi. It was nice to wear a new outfit and do her hair, to be fussed over as they enjoyed a meal someone else had cooked.

She hadn't been able to tell Andy much about the investigation that she and Jade Fitch had been involved in a few months ago. However, she could explain that learning to trust a virtual stranger had led to seizing opportunities for the Book Barge and the business was steadily growing into what she'd always planned.

And Andy, whom she'd initially met in a bereavement support group, had finally admitted that what had been eating him up was not simply the loss of his wife, but his failure to resume the professional acting career he'd put aside when she fell ill.

They had both hugged their dreams inside them, afraid to be honest. No wonder it hadn't worked out. Now Fi felt in control of the Book Barge instead of the other way round, and there was a chance that Andy's acting career would take off. So why not start again?

'Let's look at the theatre before I walk you home,' said Andy.

'I've seen the display. It's great.'

'Today?'

'No.'

'Come on then.'

In the chilly night air, Fi tucked her arm into his and leaned in for warmth. It was so bitingly cold that even the moonlight seemed icy. They turned from the old lane up the high street, past the decorated windows of Jade's shop Crystal Dreams, and made their way to the Little Theatre.

Framed with bright bulbs was the publicity information for *Macbeth*. A banner across the top said *Hazeby-on-Wyvern Autumn Arts Festival.*

'Look,' said Andy, pointing at another banner which declared that the first night was nearly sold out.

'Fantastic!' said Fi. She pointed at the main poster, a deceptively simple design incorporating a crown floating between the upraised hands of a woman whose wild hair was made of branches and daggers. 'I bet that's helped. It's wonderful, but it must have cost a fortune to commission.'

'No expense has been spared on this production,' said Andy. 'Charles is determined to transform our amateur troupe into a proper touring rep company. Presenting a professional image is part of that. Our only compromise is having the high-school drama students help out backstage.'

'I can't tell you how thrilled Dylan is,' said Fi, thinking of her fourteen-year-old son's excitement about being involved. 'They won't let you down.'

'Good,' said Andy. 'Charles has contacted top critics and theatres and so on. This afternoon he said we have some real movers and shakers coming for the opening night. Even TV people. He hasn't said who yet.' Andy put his arm round her shoulder and squeezed. 'I'm in my forties. Maybe it's too late.'

'It's never too late,' said Fi. 'Joining Charles's troupe after Ellie died saved your sanity and kept your hand in. Now it might lead to something else. TV is full of characters in their forties. This could be your moment.'

'I love the theatre, but a good TV role…'

Fi gave him a one-armed hug then stepped forward to look at the black and white photographs. As producer and director, Charles wasn't pictured, so Fi's eyes were drawn to the two other people in the troupe whom she knew reasonably well: Andy, and the woman who was usually leading lady, Charles's partner Elsa.

Andrew Hale as Macbeth. A moody shot of Andy in costume, holding a crown. Here his expression, normally friendly, was arrogant and smug.

Elsa O'Brien as Lady Macduff. An attractive woman in her late thirties with fair curls flowing under a medieval veil, and proud determination in her large eyes.

Elsa's expression of righteous anger might not be entirely acting, though, because her photograph was well down the list, instead of next to Andy's. And above them both, top of the bill, was *Tallulah Levantine as Lady Macbeth.*

If Elsa's eyes were large, Tallulah's were enormous, outlined by long, thick lashes and smudgy black kohl. If Elsa was attractive, Tallulah was beautiful: her cheekbones high, her face heart-shaped, her scheming red-lipped smile, even with a dagger touching it, luscious.

On the other hand, while Elsa's photograph was flattering and sharp, Tallulah's was unquestionably soft focus. She would never be less than lovely, but equally she would never again be less than seventy years old.

'Tallulah says the play's success is down to her presence,' said Andy moodily. 'Beauty and intelligence don't always go hand in hand.'

'They do in me,' said Fi, fluttering her eyelashes.

'I don't know what Charles was thinking. Even after all these weeks, Elsa is barely speaking to him. I feel ridiculous, "married" to a woman old enough to be my mother.'

'At least it's not *Romeo and Juliet* and there won't be kissing.' Fi tried to keep her voice neutral.

'Stop laughing.'

'You're catastrophising,' said Fi, nudging him. 'Tallulah's bound to have contacts. Hazeby Film Society gave me the titles of books about her, or including her, for me to sell on the Book Barge during the festival. There are quite a few.'

'Obscure stuff is absolute gold to film socs.' Andy still seemed gloomy as they made their way to the river. 'Admit it, you'd never heard of Tallulah before she moved to Hazeby and Charles hired her.'

'No,' said Fi. 'But I'm not a film buff. I only know blockbusters and the odd classic. Just neither of the classics that Tallulah filmed.'

'She blew her chance,' said Andy. 'They're good. Of their era, of course – psychedelic, bogus eastern symbolism, with Tallulah in a minidress and knee-high boots talking psychobabble.'

'So she's not a terrible actress.'

'She's a very good one,' said Andy. 'I'd have more time for her if she'd continued with quality productions. She could have been another Joanna Lumley: eternally beautiful, creative, talented, true to herself. A British icon. Instead, she veered into tacky seventies stuff: innuendo, pointless semi-nudity and corny horror. It's no wonder she'd more or less dropped off the radar by the eighties.'

'But if Tallulah being involved in *Mac*—'

'The Scottish play.' Andy frowned at her.

'If Tallulah being involved in the Scottish play gets you noticed…'

'I suppose,' said Andy. 'As long as no one thinks that acting with a washed-up actress is a reflection on me.'

They paused near the last street lamp while Fi changed into flat shoes. The towpath might be muddy, the gangplank to the barge slippery. Boats, darkness and high heels didn't go together.

'I've really enjoyed this evening,' said Andy, as

they resumed their walk.

'Me too.'

'I hope we can find time to see each other in spite of the festival. I know you've got things going on too.'

'Just a couple of indie author talks inside the Book Barge and the writers' group doing an open mic on the deck. We'll find time.'

They stopped where *Coralie's* gangplank rested on the towpath. Moonlight sparkled on the Wyvern's tiny waves and lamplight glowed through the curtains of the barge. Dylan would be in his cabin, but he'd have left the main light and the log burner on for Fi's return.

Andy leaned in for a kiss. Fi felt shy for a moment, then lifted her face.

Rrrerrfff?

'What?' said Andy, pulling back.

'I didn't say anything.'

Rrrerrfff.

'It's coming from the barge,' said Andy. 'Is Dylan playing the fool?'

'He wouldn't.' Was there a tiny tapping noise?

'It's Tallulah's false eyelashes going for a run,' said Andy. His laugh sounded forced.

The hairs on the back of Fi's neck rose as they turned on their phone torches and trained them on the barge. The chairs and plants looked suddenly ominous, the storage shed sinister.

At the base of the wheelhouse door, two small glinting lights.

Rrrerrfff. Then a tiny whine.

'It's a dog,' said Andy.

'What the—' Fi crossed the gangplank. The dog was small, male and shivering. He lowered his head and bared his teeth in a sort of nervous smile. His tail thumped against the wood. 'That means he wants to be friends, doesn't it?' She crouched, reached out her hand to let the dog sniff her, then touched his head. 'He's soaking wet and freezing. We can't leave him outside. Let's get him in the warm.'

'But—'

Fi unlocked the wheelhouse door and picked up the dog, hoping he wasn't muddy. She entered the boat with Andy close behind. In the light, the dog was some sort of terrier with brindled grey fur. There was no tag on his collar. Despite the warmth of the barge, he kept shivering.

'I'll get a towel,' said Fi, handing the dog to Andy.

'And maybe wine?' said Andy, his head on one side. He sat on the sofa and put the dog on the floor. 'We can cuddle up, post on the Hazeby Lost Dogs Facebook page, have a chat, then maybe—'

The dog barked his approval and licked Andy's hand.

There was a bang, and Dylan bounced into the room. 'A dog? Did you—? Oh, hello Andy. Is he yours?' He plumped himself down in the middle of the sofa. 'What's his name? I always wanted a dog but Mum said no.'

Andy grimaced at Fi. 'Maybe I'll just have a coffee and go home. I have a murder to rehearse.'

CHAPTER 2

The customer, a smallish, greyish woman buttoned up in a duffle coat, regarded Jade with a pleading expression. 'My friend said you'd definitely help me.'

Jade sighed. 'I'm not a clairvoyant.'

'But my friend said—'

'I'm not. A clairvoyant. Whatever people say.' Jade glanced at Netta, who was leaning on the counter, lips parted, taking in the action like a spectator at Wimbledon. 'What is it you want me to find again?'

The customer gave a happy little sigh and beamed at her. 'My amethyst and pearl pendant. It was a gift from my mother on my twenty-first birthday, passed down from her mother, and if I've lost it I don't know what I'll do. It isn't valuable, not really, but in sentimental terms—'

'I understand,' said Jade. She eyed the witch clock, which showed it was five minutes to one. Fi would arrive any minute. 'Where did you last see the pendant?'

'Will you put me in a trance?' the customer said eagerly.

'No,' said Jade. 'I'll just ask you some questions.'

'She always says that,' said Netta. 'That's when the magic happens.'

Jade gave Netta a look that ought to have melted her on the spot, but she appeared completely unmoved. *Where's magic when you need it*, she thought.

She faced the customer. 'Once more, where did you last see the pendant?'

'I last wore it over Christmas, when all the family were together. I tend to keep it for family occasions as it's so meaningful to me.'

Jade gazed steadily at the customer to keep from rolling her eyes. 'Do you remember putting it away? In a jewellery box, for example.'

'Oh yes, I have a jewellery box,' said the customer. 'It's ever so nice, a wooden one padded with cream silk, and it even has a little secret compartment. Well, it's not very secret. You lift the box up and press a little button on the bottom, and a drawer slides out.'

'I take it the pendant isn't in there,' said Jade.

'That was the first place I tried,' said the customer. Jade heard a small disappointed sigh some way down the shop. *I bet Derren Brown never has to put up with this sort of thing.*

However, the customer didn't seem concerned. 'I distinctly remember taking the pendant off on Boxing Day evening and putting it in the box. I was relieved to have it safe again. I always worry that the chain will break or a stone will drop out.'

'Do you ever worry that someone will steal it?' asked Jade.

'Not usually,' said the customer. 'Although after that story in the local paper – you know, about a gang going round the area burgling people while pretending to quote for cavity wall insulation – I was worried. I wouldn't let a stranger across the threshold of my house for months. I mean, it's not as if we have much to steal, certainly not that you could put in your pocket and walk off with, but it's still a worry. I remember squirrelling things away in all sorts of places. In the kitchen cupboard behind the spice rack, rolled up in a pair of socks, taped to the back of a picture—'

Jade raised her eyebrows. 'Rolled up in a pair of socks, you say?'

'Yes. Not smelly socks like sports socks, though.' The customer's face suggested that she had had dealings with many smelly socks in her life. '*Nice* socks.'

'So your pendant could be tucked inside your nicest pair of socks,' said Jade.

The customer gasped and fixed round, pale-blue eyes on Jade. 'The cashmere ones my son gave me!' she cried. 'They're so soft and beautiful that I've never dared wear them. Thank you, thank you!' She hurried to the door. 'I'll just make sure, then I'll come back and buy something.'

'I'm sure you will,' Jade said to the closing door. 'And wear your nice socks!'

'Wow,' said Netta, giving her a little round of applause.

Jade unleashed the eye roll she had been keeping in. 'There was nothing supernatural about that, Netta. All she needed was a bit of prompting.'

'Oh, but there's more to it than that, isn't there?' said a well-groomed woman, one of a trio Jade privately called the Three Witches.

Jade grinned. 'There isn't, but if it makes you happy to think so—'

The door opened. It was Fi, wrapped up in an olive-green puffer jacket teamed with a cheerful hat and scarf in autumnal colours. As she approached the counter, the witch clock cackled.

'Now that's an entrance,' said Jade. 'Netta, can you look after things while we go for lunch?'

'Course I can,' said Netta. 'And if anyone wants anything' – she leaned forward and lowered her voice – 'special—'

'They can wait until I get back,' said Jade. 'Need

anything from the shops?'

'You're OK,' said Netta. 'I'll get a pasty in a bit. And maybe a hot chocolate, with cream and marshmallows.'

Jade eyed Netta's slim figure with envy. 'Wish I could make calories disappear like that.'

A faint whine of machinery made itself heard through the gentle ambient music playing in the shop. 'For heaven's sake,' said Jade. She marched to the stereo and turned it up just as the noise stopped. 'Remind me to have a word with him when I get back, Netta. See you in an hour or so.'

***

Jade eyed Fi as they left the shop. 'You look disgustingly cheerful,' she said. 'Bright-eyed and bushy-tailed.'

'Maybe that's the benefit of having a new man in my life,' said Fi, and grinned.

Jade's eyebrows shot up. 'It was only your second date last night. It hasn't taken this Andy long to get his feet under the table, has it?' She imagined herself playing gooseberry while Fi and Andy canoodled. Maybe he was already at the pub, keeping a table for them…

Fi stared at her. 'What? No!' She smiled. 'Not that sort of new man. When we got back to the barge last night, a little dog had stowed away on board. A terrier-type dog. The poor thing was cold and soaking wet, so I took him in.'

'Oh,' said Jade. She felt rather silly, but at the same time relieved. 'Are you keeping him? I assume he doesn't have a collar or a microchip.'

'Neither,' said Fi. 'I took him to get scanned at the vet this morning and nothing. They took a photo of him and said they'd post on Facebook and stick it on their noticeboard, but they said he might have been lost for some time. He's thin and his coat is matted. And he's very hungry. He needs a bath, but I haven't worked myself up to that yet.'

'So you've got a ship's dog,' said Jade. 'I bet Dylan's pleased. What does Andy think?'

Fi grimaced. 'As far as Andy's concerned, the jury's out. Shame, really: we had a lovely evening. A meal and drinks at the Vine, and on the way back Andy took me to see the posters at the theatre.'

Jade frowned. 'Didn't he show you those the other day?'

'It wasn't like that,' said Fi. 'The play's doing well, so of course he's proud. They've practically sold out the first night.'

'Have they now?' said Jade. 'Remind me what they're doing.' She grinned.

Fi struck an attitude and a middle-aged man in a Barbour jacket gave her an incredulous look as he passed by. 'The Scottish play.'

'You mean *Macbeth*,' said Jade. 'I only know

you're not meant to mention its name because of *Blackadder*. That's the play with the witches, isn't it?'

'That's the one,' said Fi. 'Three witches and a formidable Lady Macbeth.'

'Oh yes, Tallulah Whatsits.' Jade strolled beside Fi, musing. 'Part of the arts festival, I believe. I was going to give that a miss as it didn't seem particularly relevant, but if the play's doing well... Do you mind if we take a brief detour?'

'What, to the theatre?' Fi shrugged. 'We can, if you like.'

'So...' Jade considered how to phrase her question. 'Would you be up for running a bookstall in the theatre foyer while the play's on? You could bring books on Shakespeare, acting, witchcraft, maybe history...'

'Mmm,' said Fi. 'I hadn't thought of that. And I suppose you could be persuaded to run a stall with cauldrons, spell books and silver charms.'

Jade smiled. 'Oh, I definitely could. And I bet Netta will help me with it, if the price is right.' She glanced at Fi. 'How about you? Would you rope in Nerys?'

'That's the tricky bit,' said Fi. 'I'd like to – she's very willing – but it'll be evenings and she has a young family. There's Geraldine...' She sighed.

'How are you two getting on these days? Have

Coralie's vibes improved at all?' Geraldine, Fi's Monday assistant, had never been the same since embarking on a spiritual retreat in the summer. In so doing, she had completely missed out on a dramatic murder at the book barge and the investigation which followed. 'Did I tell you that she bought a tiger's-eye necklace from me a week after she returned?'

Fi made a face. 'I'm not surprised. Not that it's made any difference to her attitude, which I presume means it hasn't dispelled the vibes.' Jade snorted. 'I have no idea what she'll say when she sees the new crew member.'

'Maybe you should cross that gangplank when you come to it,' said Jade. 'Anyway, we're almost at the theatre and their doors are open. Let's get ourselves starring roles as the best neighbourhood suppliers of spooky goods.' She paused outside the theatre, undid her long, swishy coat, straightened her spiderweb-print top and smoothed her hair, which had recently acquired purple highlights. 'Do I look all right?'

'Of course you do.'

'I mean, do I look like someone they shouldn't turn down?'

Fi laughed. 'Come on, you're everyone's favourite local witch.'

Jade huffed. 'Not a witch.'

'Wise woman, then. Uncanny person.'

Jade grinned. 'Whatever you say, boss. Let's go

in.' She strode straight into the theatre as if she owned the place, and Fi followed.

CHAPTER 3

A knock on the wheelhouse door heralded a yell of 'Post!'

Fi was in the middle of a phone conversation with her mother-in-law, Annie. She hurried up the steps, took a small pile of letters from the postman and watched him cross the gangplank and stride along the towpath. Phone pressed to one ear, she flicked through the envelopes, returned to the galley and put the kettle on.

'...so Dylan asked if we'd come on the third night, once everyone knows the ropes,' Annie was saying. 'Is "knowing the ropes" a sailing term or a theatrical one? Anyway, is that all right? Are Trisha and Pete coming?'

'Mum and Dad? No, they can't,' said Fi. 'They've an influx of end-of-season guests. The third night is perfect. You and Nigel can have my cabin.'

'Oh. Well...' Annie still disapproved of Fi giving up a corporate career for life on the Book Barge, which she thought should be kept for weekend getaways. Fi was doing her best to win her round. The fact that Fi was now respected by the police and Dylan was doing well enough at school to be involved in the theatre production was helping a good deal. At least Annie was slowly coming round to the fact that Dylan's school was a good one, even if it wasn't posh. Fi loved Annie dearly, but wished she wouldn't fuss so much or snap when she was worried. Today, however, she was quite mellow. 'I suppose we could.'

'Please do. It's much nicer than a hotel full of tourists,' Fi said. 'I'll stay at a friend's. You can have a little holiday on the boat, spoil Dylan to your heart's content and feed him whatever you like.'

A pause, then a chuckle. 'All right. What about the dog?'

'Ah. Dylan's told you.'

'It's de-fleaed, I hope.'

'The vet did the necessary,' said Fi. 'He's young and healthy, apart from being underweight, but there's no microchip and no owner has come forward yet. I don't want to put him in a shelter until I have to. It's freezing, and he's...'

Fi looked down at the dog, who peered up with a trusting gaze. 'Rrrerrfff.' He was wolfish in colouring but slightly soppy-looking, and he couldn't bark properly. *He might get beaten up by tougher dogs,* she thought, then: *Don't get sentimental, Fi. Someone will collect him any day.*

'I bet you've named him.'

Just in my head. There's no point getting attached. 'Sorry, Annie, I'll have to go. Jade's coming in a moment to plan our stall layouts in the theatre foyer.'

'Your crystal friend?'

'Yes.' Fi braced herself for mutterings about New Age nonsense. The only thing Annie tended to be sentimental, unrealistic or whimsical about was her dead son, Gavin.

'Can you ask her to save an amethyst bracelet for me?'

Fi's eyes widened. 'I didn't think crystals were your sort of thing.'

'Wait till you get arthritis,' said Annie. 'You'll try anything. If it doesn't work, at least it'll be pretty. Bye.'

Fi put the phone down and applied herself to the mail. It was all business correspondence, except one envelope which had been forwarded from the house she'd sold four years previously, before setting up the Book Barge. The house she'd lived in with Gavin, until he'd left her with a small child, then died in a car accident abroad.

Something about the writing on the original address seemed familiar: spiky but feminine capitals, slightly slanted. Fi opened the envelope and extracted a newspaper clipping with a large sticky note attached.

Hi Fi,

Me and Stefan thought we saw Gavin's ghost when we were on our hols in Italy. Just as well we got someone to translate the article or we'd have gone and sorted him out. Proves what they say, everyone's got a double. Thought you'd want to see. What a laugh!

Mel

The clipping showed a group of men who'd won a trophy. One of them, half hidden by another, looked like Fi's dead husband, only pixelated. For a moment, she felt sick. Then she felt angry.

Underneath were a string of Italian names. She counted them, then counted the men. The same number. She stared at the photograph. It wasn't even that much like Gavin. It was just Mel being spiteful.

Some people would say she's justified, thought Fi, scowling. *Gavin owed enough of his friends money. But I remortgaged the house to pay them all off. What more could I do? And what kind of person sends a photograph of someone who resembles a dead man to his widow? I never liked her in the first place. It's as well she doesn't know where I live now.*

'What did that piece of paper ever do to you?' said Jade, climbing into the boat. 'If you crumple it any more it'll turn to dust.'

Fi stared at the ball of newspaper, growled, and chucked it into the kindling basket beside the log burner.

'Good shot,' said Jade.

'Goal shooter on the school netball team.'

'You would be. Still doesn't explain why you were squishing it so hard.'

'It's a long story. I'll tell you over lunch, if you're up for it. Nerys will be here in a moment and we should get cracking. Tea?'

Jade nodded. 'Builders' tea, please. None of that herbal nonsense. I need my brain to work.'

Fi grinned as they went into the galley, leaving the door ajar. 'Don't let your customers hear that: they'd be disappointed. Talking of customers, my mother-in-law wants an amethyst bracelet to ward off arthritis. Or just to look nice. Both, preferably.'

'Really? I'll put one aside,' said Jade as she sat down at the table. 'But I make no promises.'

'Annie knows that.'

'Aw, hello dog. Yes, I like you too, but I keep telling you I'm a cat person. No, there isn't room on my lap. You can't squeeze up— Oh, you can. No, you can't lick my earrings. Get your tongue out of my ear! Stop it!'

Fi grinned as Jade and the dog wrestled, a flurry of bangles and purple scarf with a tail beating in the midst, then whistled. The dog jumped down and stood at Fi's feet, his head on one side.

'Basket,' she said, delivering their tea and pointing at the small bed she'd made up. 'Jade and I have work to do.'

With the canine equivalent of a shrug, the dog lay down and chewed a dog toy in the shape of a ghost that Dylan had bought from Crystal Dreams.

'I'm not sure I approve of your new man,' said Jade, unfolding a large sheet of paper and spreading it on the table. 'He's very forward.'

'He's lovely.' Fi opened her tablet.

'Are we still talking about the dog?' said Jade, with narrowed eyes.

'That would be telling.'

'Mmm. So are your in-laws coming for opening night?'

'No, thank goodness,' said Fi. 'I'm cooking dinner for Andy to celebrate.'

'With Dylan as chaperone?'

'Dylan will stay at his friend's. It'll just be the two of us. Unless you fancy being chaperone?'

'Bleurgh,' said Jade. 'Guard your own honour.' She arranged the marker pens she'd brought into a pentangle.

Fi smiled. 'When the show's finished—'

'You and Andy are going on a mini break.'

'No. I'm making you and me a meal to celebrate all the sales we'll have made. I might even bake a cake.'

Jade stared at the tiny stove. '*Can* you?'

'OK, I'll buy one.'

'Won't you want to celebrate with Andy?'

'We've only been going out five minutes,' said Fi. 'We're not joined at the hip.'

'I'll drink to that.' Jade clinked mugs. 'Having dinner, I mean.'

For the next hour, Nerys managed book sales in the main part of the boat while Fi and Jade, using lots of sticky notes, worked out how to arrange their tables, what they'd sell and how they'd support each other. The sheet of paper looked as if it had square measles by the time Nerys poked her head into the private quarters. 'Jon Angel's here to see you, Fi.'

'Who?' whispered Jade. Fi shrugged.

'And his team,' Nerys continued. 'They've got phones the size of laptops and one's doing *this* with his hands.' She demonstrated making a frame with her fingers and looking through it.

'Pretending to be a camera?' said Fi. 'Why? Please tell me it's not journalists wanting to discuss what happened in the summer.'

Nerys handed over a business card: *Jon Angel, Producer.*

'Who?' whispered Jade, leaning forward and reading upside down.

'Don't you read the *Gazette*?' said Nerys. 'They're filming *Meadows of Murder* in Finchampton! You know, the whodunnit series. Jon Angel's the producer. Liam's mate's an extra: "man in crowd". I wish it was me. I could be "woman in crowd". Probably with a pushchair.'

Fi and Jade exchanged glances and went into the main part of the boat.

Jon Angel appeared to be in his late sixties: older than Fi had expected. However, what she knew about TV producers could be written on the head of a pin. He was medium-height, with the physique of someone who worked out, a full head of grey hair and piercing blue eyes. He stood, hands in pockets, looking round *Coralie* as if he was about to make an offer no one could refuse.

In a way, he was.

'An extra told one of the cast about your barge,' he said, as they shook hands.

Nerys nudged Fi.

'How lovely,' said Fi, wondering what had been said. 'I don't have a big film and TV section, but—'

'That isn't why I'm here, Ms Booker,' said Jon. He scanned the boat again, blinking at Jade, then fixing Fi with an appraising stare. 'I want a location. I'd have called this barge the perfect place for a murder, but...' He gave a booming laugh that made Fi jump. 'I gather you wouldn't like that.'

'Erm...' said Fi. 'Perhaps not.'

'But as the home of an eccentric...' Once more his gaze paused on Jade. '*That* would be excellent.'

'Not an eccentric suspect, I hope,' said Jade, her eyes narrowed.

Jon recoiled slightly. 'I was thinking of an expert witness. All these books, all this knowledge... It would just be a set, you understand. I'm not asking you to act. We'd pay well. And of course, the Book Barge would get *good* publicity.'

'Can I think about it?' said Fi.

'Of course. I wouldn't expect you to answer straight away.' Jon tapped on his phone. 'Wyvernshire's a lovely county. I can't believe I'd never been to Hazeby before. It's perfect: very picturesque. Odd to have bunting at this time of year, but pretty anyway.'

'An arts festival is starting soon,' said Jade.

'Really?'

'There's a production of *Macbeth*,' said Fi, handing him a flyer. Then she winced. 'Sorry, the Scottish play.'

'It's only unlucky to name it in a theatre, I believe,' said Jon. He took the flyer and raised his eyebrows. 'Tallulah Levantine? That's a blast from the past. I've often wondered what happened to her.'

'I have books about Ms Levantine on order,' said Fi. 'They'll be on sale at the theatre.'

Jon's booming laugh rang out. He clicked his fingers at his team then shook hands with Fi. 'I hope you'll consider my suggestion, Ms Booker. Perhaps we can discuss it at the Little Theatre.'

'So you'll come?' Fi tried to look nonchalant. If Jon Angel was as big a deal as Nerys thought, maybe, if he saw Andy acting…

'Oh yes,' said Jon. 'It would be worth going to see Tallulah again. It'll be a night to remember.'

CHAPTER 9

Jade returned to the shop to find Netta gazing at a book propped open on the counter and brandishing an incense stick. 'What are you doing, exactly?' she asked.

Netta jumped and gave her a reproachful look. 'I was practising,' she said. 'I thought it would be better to use a stick than a wand. I didn't want to do any damage.'

Jade picked up the book and inspected the cover: *Spells for Beginners*. 'Ah, one of our best sellers.' She put the book down and studied Netta. 'You do realise it's twaddle, don't you?'

Netta's mouth dropped open. 'I can't believe you're saying that. You, a magic-shop owner, in front of all this...' She made a sweeping gesture and Jade stepped back hastily to avoid a stick-related injury. 'This *stuff*.'

Jade sighed. 'This is a profitable business, Netta. If people choose to believe in this sort of thing I can't stop them, and at least they can't buy anything dangerous here.' She eyed the incense stick. 'Well, not intentionally dangerous.'

She gazed around the shop. It was quiet, apart from two young women whispering by the cauldrons and a woman muffled up in coat, scarf and hat who seemed intent on the book display. 'Anything interesting happen while I was out?'

Netta shook her head. 'The usual, really. We had a few people in, but some said they'd come back later. I think they want to see you.' She pouted.

'Is that why you're having a go with the book?' Jade asked, as kindly as she could.

Netta hung her head. 'S'pose.'

'Oh, Netta.' Jade considered patting her arm, but Netta didn't welcome that sort of thing. 'I'm sure that once people are used to you, they won't care who serves them. Now, why don't you take a break? You must be hungry, and a bit of fresh air and a walk will do you good.' *You sound like her mother*, she thought. *Or possibly grandma.*

'Maybe,' said Netta, and dawdled her way to the back room.

'Could you make me a brew while you're there?' Jade called after her, and received a shrug in reply.

She installed herself behind the counter. *I should*

check my stock. I bet anything witchy or Scottish will sell like hot cakes in the theatre. Is there a Macbeth tartan? She took out her phone, opened the browser, and searched. *Gosh, that's bright.*

A movement in the shop attracted Jade's attention. The bundled-up customer was watching the back-room door. *What's that about?* Jade was about to ask if she needed help when the shop door opened and a petite figure glided in.

Jade recognised her immediately, though she had never seen her in the flesh before. She was wearing a long leather coat and knee-high boots, and a pink scarf was draped artistically round her throat in a way that Jade couldn't have achieved in a month of Sundays. Her hair was long and honey blonde, with paler strands framing her face. The clincher, perhaps, was that she was wearing sunglasses in October, despite the cloudy day. She removed them and flashed a megawatt smile. *That's Tallulah Levantine. It couldn't be anyone else.* In comparison with the photograph of her which had top billing at Hazeby Little Theatre, however, she looked more like Tallulah Levantine's mother.

'Good afternoon,' said Tallulah. 'I wonder if you could help me. I'm in town for the production – the Scottish play – and I'm looking for some . . . accessories.'

Netta came out of the back room and stopped

dead. 'It's her,' she murmured, then 'It's you!'

'Indeed it is, daahling,' said Tallulah, extending a hand with long, dusky-pink nails. *Bet those turn red for the production.*

Netta hurried forward, cradled Tallulah's hand as if it were a baby bird, and dipped in a sort of curtsey. Tallulah regarded her in the manner of a merciful queen.

Jade waited for a moment, and when nothing happened, cleared her throat. 'What sort of thing would you be looking for, Ms Levantine?'

'Oh, call me Tallulah. Everyone does, daahling. No airs and graces here, I assure you.' Her laugh tinkled like a music box. 'I don't know if you've seen the posters, but I am taking on the role of Lady Macbeth, and it's so important to get the details right.'

'Oh, I see.' Jade picked up Netta's book from the counter. 'Well, if you were interested in the right way to make magical gestures, for instance...'

'Oh yes,' said Tallulah. She drew herself up to what Jade estimated was her full five foot two, even in heeled boots, lifted her arm, and spread her fingers. 'Perhaps a cloak... I'll have to ask the costume department.'

'Might I suggest a tartan shawl?' said Jade. 'There's a specific Macbeth one, and it would show your character's commitment to the clan. You could drape it over one shoulder, and use it in various ways.'

She showed Tallulah her phone.

'I looooove stagecraft,' Tallulah purred. 'Could you possibly order something like that for me, daahling?'

'Of course,' said Jade. 'If I take your number, I can let you know when it comes in. Or deliver it to the theatre, of course.'

'I could do that,' said Netta. 'It wouldn't be any trouble.'

'How kind of you,' said Tallulah. 'I was worried that, coming back to Hazeby after so many years and no longer in my prime, I might be – not unwelcome, but *overlooked*.' She pouted, and suddenly resembled Netta. 'It's such a relief.' Then she grimaced and looked more like a naughty schoolgirl. 'Now there's just the Scottish play to fret about.'

'You mustn't fret, Tallulah,' said Netta. 'You're a star.'

'Absolutely,' said Jade. 'But if you are interested in a good-luck charm to keep evil away, we do have several. Netta, would you mind introducing Tallulah to our selection?'

'I'd be delighted,' breathed Netta, and she ushered Tallulah towards a shelf where a variety of silver charms hung on black ribbons and leather thongs. 'We have a cat, a four-leaf clover, a horseshoe, and this is a rabbit's foot... Replica, of course, not real.'

'That looks exactly like something Lady Macbeth

would have,' said Tallulah, unhooking the rabbit's foot.

'Um, Tallulah, would you mind if I took a photo of you with Netta?' asked Jade.

'Oh, please do,' pleaded Netta. 'It would mean the world to me.'

'Of course,' said Tallulah. She stood side-on, one foot in front of the other, put an arm round Netta, and flung up her chin. An enigmatic smile played around her red lips. Jade wondered why she didn't unleash the megawatt smile, but suspected it was because of laughter lines.

Tallulah held her pose while Jade snapped a few pictures. 'May I see?' Jade brought the phone for her to inspect. 'Marvellous. You can put a copy up in the shop, too.'

'Could we post a photo on our social media?' asked Netta.

Tallulah tinkled. 'Whatever you like, daahling.' She released Netta, who rubbed her arm surreptitiously. 'Shall I sign a few things while I'm here?'

Jade wished she had followed her gut instinct to order in some copies of *Macbeth*. 'If you wouldn't mind, perhaps a spell book or two...'

'Of course!' Tallulah rummaged in her bag, produced an expensive-looking pen, then signed whatever Jade brought her with a flourish. 'There,' she said. 'I hope they bring you business.'

'I'm sure they will,' said Jade. 'From one independent woman to another, thank you.' *I'll get those Macbeths ordered, tip off Fi, and maybe when Tallulah's shawl arrives…*

Tallulah put her pen in her bag and heaved a theatrical sigh. 'It's hard work, though, isn't it? Being an independent woman. There's always someone out to get you. I mean, here's little old me, quite past it, and yet some – person – wrote me a nasty note.' Her eyebrows drew together in the tiniest of frowns. '*Give up and get out or die*, it said! How melodramatic! Unsigned, of course: these things always are.'

Jade raised her eyebrows. 'You should report that to the police, Tallulah. There are odd people out there.'

Tallulah waved a hand in dismissal. 'Oh no, it's nonsense. The police would laugh at me. I mean, it's no more than a bad review, and I've had plenty of those in my time.'

'Mmm,' said Jade. 'I still think you should report it.'

'You should listen to Jade, Tallulah,' said Netta. 'She's solved a murder. And she's got powers.'

Jade gave Netta a resigned look. 'Netta, I don't have powers.'

'I know what I've seen,' said Netta. 'And you did solve a murder, anyway.'

'Gosh,' said Tallulah, tinkling again. 'Maybe *you* should be in the play. What do I owe you?' She paid, waited for Netta to wrap her purchases, and wafted out of the shop.

'Well, that was exciting,' said Jade, 'I'll send you that photo, Netta, but don't post it anywhere without my say-so.'

'Can I show my friends?'

'Of course. Now go and get your lunch.'

Netta eyed Jade, then stood on tiptoe and gave her a very quick hug. 'Thank you,' she muttered.

'Steady on!' said Jade.

'I didn't squeeze too hard, did I?' Netta looked rather worried. 'That Tallulah might be . . . mature, but she's got a proper grip on her.'

'Don't worry, I'm a tough old bird,' said Jade. 'Make sure you take your full hour, that's probably the most excitement we'll get today.'

Jade watched Netta go, and when she turned back to the shop she realised someone else had been watching Netta too. The bundled-up stranger. Only she wasn't a stranger. Her face had been hidden before, but now Jade recognised her.

Fi's Monday assistant, Geraldine.

CHAPTER 5

On opening night Fi and Dylan made their way into town, both lost in their own thoughts.

Fi contemplated Dylan out of the corner of her eye. He was uncharacteristically silent. Perhaps something had gone wrong that she had no way of knowing about: an unrequited love, an imagined slight. When you were a teenager, any disappointment or humiliation seemed overwhelming. Or maybe it was working in a theatre, where there were even more superstitions than there were on boats. Not that she knew much about either, or thought Dylan would care.

'What's up?' she said. 'Aren't you enjoying being backstage?'

Dylan stared. 'It's great! I'm loving every minute. Charles is great, too – he got a couple of old stagehands to train us properly. Only…'

'The actors?'

Dylan hesitated. 'Andy and Elsa are a bit serious and Old Tom, who plays Duncan, is *really* up himself. The three witches are a laugh. I never thought they could be cast as young women before. Max fancies Beth, though he swears he doesn't.' He sniggered. 'Barty Sheen overacts the Porter a bit, but then he's Andy's understudy, so perhaps it's to prove he could step up if you poison Andy with your cooking tonight.'

'Thanks.'

'I've told the dog to make sure you don't get up to anything disgusting. You're too old for that sort of thing.' He shuddered.

'Huh,' said Fi. 'Have you told Nana I'm seeing Andy? You've told her about the dog.'

'A dog's different.' Dylan waved at another shivering teenager wearing a *CREW* T-shirt but no coat, going in the opposite direction.

Fi grimaced to herself. *What did that mean?* 'How do you get on with Tallulah?'

'She's cool. Calls us all daahhling and buys us sweets. She does yoga every day and she can do the splits. Bet you can't.'

'I don't want to.'

'She told us about filming when it was more laid back and experimental. Dodgy props, smoking on set, people doing their own stunts...'

'More dangerous?'

'Yeah,' Dylan conceded. 'But more fun. I expect that's why she's not been too bothered.'

'Too bothered about what?'

'The accidents.'

Fi grabbed Dylan's arm and pulled him to a halt. 'What accidents?'

'Don't fuss.' Dylan rubbed his arm.

'I'm not. I'm asking a question.'

'One of the goblets was damaged and nearly cut her hand,' said Dylan, after a short silence. 'That was the first thing. Then something was left on the floor and she tripped. If she hadn't righted herself, she *might* have fallen on one of the swords.'

'Those sort of things could happen to anyone,' said Fi. 'I can trip over my own shadow some days. And aren't they collapsible swords?'

'It's not a kids' show,' said Dylan, with scorn. 'They're blunt. Tallulah said that it was because one of the background actors called the play by its name. She forced Charles to make him leave the theatre, spin round three times, spit, make a blood-curdling curse, then knock on the door before she'd let him back in.'

Fi raised her eyebrows, but Dylan had stopped looking at her. 'There's something else, isn't there?'

Dylan stared at his feet, then addressed the nearby building in a whisper. 'A light fell from a gantry when she was crossing the stage yesterday morning,' he said. 'It just missed her.'

'Good grief! Why didn't you say? Why didn't your teacher say?'

'She doesn't know: she was stuck in traffic. Only a couple of us were there. We agreed we wouldn't tell her in case she stopped us doing the play.'

'Dylan . . . it wasn't one of you who fixed it to the gantry, was it? Is that why you're worried?'

'Gee, thanks, Mum. Just call me an idiot, why don't you?' Dylan glared at her.

'That's not what I meant.'

'Who'd let a bunch of schoolkids up a gantry?' he snapped. 'The Little Theatre's got professional guys for that sort of thing. They swore it was OK. Then Tallulah said she'd popped back into the theatre the previous night and someone had forgotten to leave the ghost light on. She said a ghost must have untied it.'

'What's a ghost light?'

'You always have to leave a light on in a theatre to keep the ghost happy.'

'Dylan…'

'Yeah, yeah,' he said, with a shrug. 'But she said she'd leave if Charles didn't sort things out, and the prop guy got fired. Or at least, asked not to come in for a few days. I think Charles will let him back in if he keeps a low profile. Don't say anything, Mum. Don't make a fuss. Three people are checking everything three times every three hours. Honest.'

Fi contemplated his woebegone face and wished she could ruffle his hair or pull him into a hug. Instead, she nodded and they parted at the main doors of the theatre. Dylan went down the narrow lane to the stage door and she entered the foyer.

Jade was putting the finishing touches to her stall as she chatted to Charles. He was weighing a crystal ball in his hands in a way that suggested he planned to lob it across the room. Jade, wearing a fixed smile, was twisting her tartan broomstick scarf into knots. Fi knew the ball was real crystal and fairly expensive. Its saleability would be greatly diminished if it were chipped.

Tallulah was at Fi's stall, disorganising the display of books.

'Oh hello, daahling,' she said, air-kissing Fi's cheeks as if they'd known each other since a childhood at St Tropez. 'What a *lovely* range you have. I've just tweaked the order a *little* bit. Call me vain if you will, but this one has the best picture of me on the cover, and this one has the best chapter about me. If any of my fans do come in, these will be what they expect to see.'

'I'll bear that in mind,' said Fi. She looked at the older woman. Under the thick make-up and Botox, it was impossible to tell if Tallulah was worried. 'Actually,' Fi said. 'I wonder if you could help me.' She indicated a book on theatre superstitions. 'Do actors really believe in all this? If something frightening happened to me on stage, I'd call the police.'

Tallulah's expression flickered and her hand, touching a book, trembled. 'Would you, daahling?'

'Yes. Even if it turned out to be nothing, it's better to be safe than sorry.'

'Oh, but…' Tallulah straightened up and brushed a nonexistent strand of hair from her lovely face. 'Don't worry, daahling. I'm not sure what you've heard, but the worst dress rehearsal always means the best opening night. One wouldn't want to stop the show from going on. That *would* upset the theatre ghosts!' She chuckled and swept towards the auditorium, passing Andy as he came to greet Fi.

'What was she saying?' he asked.

'She seemed worried about something that happened in rehearsals,' said Fi.

'Ah. Someone forgot to leave the ghost light on. It was inevitable. But it's sorted now.'

Fi stared at him. Was he serious?

'Either that, or a rusty piece of wire.' He kissed her. 'I have to go. I'm looking forward to supper tonight. Still just the two of us?'

'And the dog.'

'I can live with that.'

'Break a leg.'

'Thanks!'

After a final kiss, he turned, tapped Charles on the shoulder, and they went into the auditorium.

Fi and Jade rearranged their stalls, then dragged their chairs together and sat talking quietly. It was half an hour until the doors would open and a little over an hour before the audience would be allowed into the auditorium.

The tension in the air whispered from backstage to foyer. Everyone in the theatre was waiting, making their last checks and saying their last prayers. But in no time, the magic would begin.

***

At half past nine, the audience poured into the foyer. People emerged dazed and silent, then burst into excited chatter.

Fi and Jade had had to miss the end of the play to return to their stalls, but up to that point the performance had stunned and moved them. On stage, Tallulah was both chilling and pitiable. Andy had embodied a character consumed by his own greed, manipulated and ultimately destroyed by his belief in fate.

'She did well for an old ham,' said Jon Angel, as the foyer started to empty. He was flicking through one of Fi's Tallulah books. 'I wonder how much truth there is in this? Anyway, I'll have it. Cheap at half the price.' He tucked the book under his arm and waved a card over the machine. 'Any more thoughts about letting us use your boat for filming?'

'I'm interested,' said Fi. 'Perhaps you could come down tomorrow and discuss it.'

'Delighted. Right, I'm off to chat with Charles. I knew him when he was a whippersnapper of a stagehand.'

'Talking of stagehands...' But Jon had gone.

After covering their tables ready for the next day, Fi and Jade left and walked towards Crystal Dreams.

'A light missed her by inches and she doesn't want to tell the police?' said Jade. 'Is she mad?'

'Andy says it was a rusty wire and everything's been triple checked.'

'Triple, huh? How witchy.'

'Well, it's working. Nothing went wrong tonight: it was a rip-roaring success. I heard a reporter calling his paper.'

'The *Gazette?* Only Nerys reads that. Fi...'

'It wasn't the *Gazette*. It was a bigger paper than that.'

'I'm still worried.' It was hard to tell with nothing but street light but Jade seemed tense.

'You did all right tonight, didn't you?' said Fi. 'It looked as if your stuff was selling like hot cakes.'

'Hot mystic Scottish shortcakes. In fact, that's an idea: I might have a witch-shaped biscuit cutter. But —'

'It doesn't stop you worrying about Tallulah.

You're right. We must encourage her to at least *tell* the police.'

'Good. You agree.'

'It'll have to wait till tomorrow, though. Here we are at yours. I can't stop: I have an after-show supper to cook.'

'Won't lurve stop any hunger?'

'Very funny.'

They gave each other a swift hug and Fi hurried to the barge. The night wasn't as cold as it had been, but it was cold enough. She dashed in and put the oven on to warm up the lasagne she'd prepared earlier, then changed into a soft, flattering dress and turned up the log burner.

She was suddenly stricken with doubt. Would lasagne be a bit garlicky? Did it matter? Well, it was too late now. What music did Andy like? She couldn't remember all of a sudden.

Checking her hair and make-up in the mirror, she rolled her eyes at her reflection. *Stop behaving like a teenager,* she told herself. *You've done this before. Choose your own music. He'll have to lump it.*

Time passed until it was a quarter of an hour after she'd expected Andy to arrive. It was unusual for him to be late. She turned the oven low and checked her phone. Another ten minutes went by.

Fi put a wrap over her shoulders and went on deck. The moon had gone behind a cloud and it was hard to see. The town glowed a few metres away. Deck lights twinkled on the boats moored at the water's edge. Then...

She could just make out someone bundled up in a winter coat, head down, hurrying along the path that led to the river and *Coralie*. Fi let out the breath she'd been holding and rehearsed what she would say. She was about to go below and arrange her face into a 'Gosh, is it that time already? I had no idea you were late' expression when the figure paused, looked towards the riverboats, then scurried into the shadows and out of sight.

A second later, her phone vibrated. *Sorry, I can't make it. Something's come up.*

She messaged back. *What's wrong? Can I help?*

No. It's nothing important. Really sorry. Andy xxx

Fi stared at the message. Was that it? *Something's come up?* Nothing important, but important enough to break a date? And how like a man to think a row of typed kisses would make all the difference.

She slammed back into the wheelhouse and locked the door, then stomped through to the galley, opened the wine and poured herself a large glass. The dog looked up with a quizzical woof.

'Fancy some lasagne?' she said. 'Then maybe I'll let you sleep at the end of my bed. The end, mind. I might not be kissing you, but I'll still be able to smell the garlic.'

CHAPTER 6

Jade let herself in and stomped up the first few steps to her flat, then remembered she could probably be heard next door and switched to tiptoeing. At least her next-door neighbour wasn't playing rock music. Or if he was, he was doing it quietly.

She unlocked the top door, hung up her coat and keys, and went to the kitchenette to make tea. Next door, the gentle twang of a guitar picked out a melody. She strode across the room and turned the TV on. *There.*

It's not his fault, I suppose, she thought, as she filled the kettle, thumped it down and switched it on. *He can't help the walls being paper thin.*

As soon as she had seen someone moving in next door, Jade had rearranged her flat so that her bed and her sofa were as far from the connecting wall as possible. Not long afterwards, the newcomer had visited Crystal Dreams. 'I thought I should introduce myself,' he said. 'I'm moving into the shop and the flat next door. My name's Rick. Pleased to meet you.'

His hand was large, tanned, with square-tipped fingers. Capable. Jade shook it, half-expecting a bone-crushing grip. 'I'm Jade,' she said. 'I run this place and live over the shop.'

'Oh, right.' Rick gazed around the shop, which gave Jade the opportunity to study him. He wore the same leather jacket as when he had come to check out the shop, some weeks before. At the time she had been busy with other matters, and paid him little attention. Now she sized him up: tall, broad-shouldered, though with a bit of a tummy under his Ramones T-shirt. His hair was mostly grey and tending towards shagginess.

He turned back to her. 'Looks interesting.'

'It is,' said Jade.

'So, are you into all this? Spells and pentangles and . . . things?'

Jade wasn't sure what to say. 'Are you?'

He smiled. 'Not particularly. Music's more my thing.'

'Rock, I assume,' said Jade, nodding at the T-shirt.

'Sometimes, but I like a bit of folk too. Fairport Convention, Kate Rusby. You know.'

Jade didn't really. 'Whatever sort of music you like, I should warn you that these buildings aren't well insulated, so if you don't mind keeping it down...'

Rick's eyebrows lifted slightly. 'OK. Um, I'll get going then.'

Jade felt rather rude. 'What sort of shop are you opening?' she asked.

'I'm a furniture restorer. Woodwork, some refinishing, and I do picture framing on the side.' He paused. 'I'll sandpaper as quietly as I can, so I don't disturb you.' And that, more or less, had been that.

To be fair, Rick wasn't a particularly noisy neighbour. Mostly, Jade turned up the volume on the stereo downstairs and muttered 'Don't mess with my ambiance.'

Occasionally, though, whirring, hammering, or a high-pitched whine made its way through the thin walls. The other day, Jade had told Netta to go round and drop a hint. 'He likes you,' she said, not that she knew if Rick did or not.

'Do I have to?' whined Netta, which was almost as annoying as the sound of machinery.

'Yes!' Jade cried. 'I'm not putting up with that racket a minute longer.'

The noise next door had stopped at once. Jade waited, but it did not resume. After half an hour, she made an excuse to nip out and peeped in next door. Rick was sitting at the counter, lips pursed in what she assumed was a whistle, smoothing a wooden carving with a piece of sandpaper. *At least he's not dead*, thought Jade, and walked on.

She came to with a start and looked at her mug. The kettle had switched itself off. She set it to boil again and fetched milk from the fridge. *I ought to be over the moon*, she thought. *A night out and a successful evening's selling, with the prospect of more to come.*

The kettle rumbled its way to a crescendo. Jade made tea, got a couple of chocolate Hobnobs from the biscuit barrel, and sat down on the sofa to review the evening.

It had gone well, no doubt about it. The play had been excellent: she would never have thought that the cast, apart from Tallulah, were amateurs. Maybe she was right that a bad dress rehearsal meant a good performance. *She's been in the business long enough to know what's what.*

And the stall couldn't have gone better. Jade had taken the plunge and bought a few of the Macbeth tartan shawls, one of which Tallulah modelled so obligingly during the play, and two were snapped up in the interval. Admittedly, the buyers both mentioned that the theatre was draughty, but Jade still prided herself on her business acumen. Spell books, miniature cauldrons and wands had flown off her table. She had hinted to Fi as well, who had stocked up on several nice editions of *Macbeth* and got them signed by Tallulah, Andy, and Charles.

Tallulah and Charles had dashed off careless squiggles which might have been anything, but Andy had taken his time, sitting down to the job and signing each book with great care, writing a quote from the play above his name: *Something wicked this way comes…*

Fi had watched Andy proudly, though not in the manner of someone who fancied the pants off him. *There's nothing wrong with him*, thought Jade. *Quite a snappy dresser, seems nice.* She had expected him to be a bit wet in the play, but he had seemed another person entirely, so much so that she forgot he was Fi's boyfriend. *Which is kind of the point.*

Jade took a swig from her mug, dunked her Hobnob, and took a bite. *Maybe I'm just jealous. Fi's got a new squeeze, and Dylan, and the Book Barge is doing well. It'll do even better if Jon Angel uses it as a setting in Meadows of Murder. I'll have to queue up to talk to her, the way she's going.*

She finished her biscuit. *Crystal Dreams is doing really well too. I've got Netta to help, who's coming on, and she's sort of company. And Hugo doesn't mind when I FaceTime him for a chat. Not that he should. I mean, I'm his mum—*

A metallic clatter made her jump. Once the shops were closed the high street of Hazeby-on-Wyvern tended to be quiet, at least until people began leaving the pubs. Even then, you were more likely to hear conversations about whatever show was big on Netflix, or what people fancied for dinner the next day, than raucous singing or a shouting match.

In the street, a man in a long coat stared at a tin can. He strode towards it, scooped it up and dropped it in a nearby bin. He pushed back his hair, stood for a moment, then continued walking. Something about him was familiar. Despite the dashing coat, he was short and round-shouldered. It was too dark for Jade to make out his features, but he was nearing one of the mock-Victorian street lamps, which gave out an authentically dim light.

As the man approached the lamp, Jade saw a mop of red-gold hair and a sharp nose. Charles, of course, the play's director. She continued to observe him. He was walking quickly, as if he wanted to get somewhere, but looking around all the while. *As if he thinks he's being watched.* Instinctively, Jade pulled the curtain half across. She smiled. *He's probably full of adrenaline – the opening night of a play must be stressful. He probably needs a couple of pints, a good chat, and a kebab on the way home.* She frowned. *Where's Elsa? I'd have thought they'd be together.* She shrugged and ate her other biscuit. *And he's got it all to do again tomorrow. As have I.*

***

Jade struggled awake. Her radio alarm was blaring, and she buried her head beneath the quilt. Then her brain registered that even with her eyes closed, the room was light. 'Darn,' she murmured. She grabbed her phone from the bedside table and brought it under the covers. 8:45. *Oh no.*

Yawning, she threw back the quilt and padded to the bathroom for a two-minute shower. *I need something to wake me up properly. Otherwise I won't make it through till lunch, never mind a full day in the shop and an evening in the theatre.*

She got dressed, bunched her hair into a ponytail and set off down the road to Betsy's. *A strong coffee and a bacon roll*, she thought. *Kill or cure.*

While Jade wasn't often out at this time of day, the high street seemed busier than usual. People were stopping to chat to each other, instead of saying hello in passing. A couple of people said hello to Jade, but she was too intent on getting her breakfast to pause for a catch-up.

Typically, the queue outside Betsy's was longer than usual and moving more slowly. Jade sighed and joined the end of it. *It's not the end of the world if the shop opens at quarter past. Given the money you took last night, you've no need to worry. Though I expected more people to sleep in.*

She tuned into the conversation in front of her. 'It's terrible,' said a woman with teased blonde hair, wearing a shiny black mac. 'So violent. What a way to go. The poor man.'

Jade felt the hairs on the back of her neck rising. She moved a little further forward.

'Yes,' agreed her companion, a brunette who looked as if she was on her way to the office. 'I mean, stabbed, actually stabbed. With a dagger.'

Jade relaxed. Of course, they were talking about the play.

'I wonder who did it,' said Shiny Mac.

'Um, that would be Macbeth,' said Jade. 'But it happens offstage.'

Both women stared at her. 'What do you mean?' said Shiny Mac.

The brunette nudged her. 'She's the woman from the witch shop. *You* know.' She turned to Jade. 'Have you had a vision?' she asked earnestly.

Jade laughed. 'No, I was in the audience last night. For *Macbeth*.'

The brunette leaned towards her friend, not taking her eyes off Jade. 'She doesn't know,' she muttered.

Jade frowned. 'I don't know what?'

Shiny Mac's eyes gleamed. 'There's been a murder,' she murmured, though no one seemed to be listening. 'A real one, at the theatre. The cleaner found him this morning when she came in. Not one of the cast: a TV person, Jon something. He was in one of the dressing rooms, and he'd been stabbed with a dagger.'

CHAPTER 7

Fi hadn't been able to switch her phone off, because that would mean Dylan couldn't get in touch if he needed to. She put it on silent mode, and after drinking more wine than she'd intended, fell into a dreamless sleep while the dog lay on the floor. He showed no inclination for jumping on the bed.

She woke once at two am, startled for a second by the soft snoring in her room. She reached out for the other side of the bed, then remembered and peered over the edge to see the shadowy outline of the dog curled up on the floor, breathing steadily. Disappointment and comfort fought for control, but in the end, comfort won. The dog was good, undemanding company. He wouldn't let her down.

She checked her phone to find no messages, other than a baffled-face emoji from Dylan to her outpouring of affection and pride after the third glass of wine. Then she fell asleep again.

At seven forty-five Fi woke, foggy and apprehensive. She sat up, rubbed her eyes, and checked her phone. No messages.

Her fingers hovered above the screen. Perhaps she'd been unfair to Andy. Maybe 'it's nothing important' was a typical British male understatement meaning 'help' which she shouldn't have ignored. But there'd been no hint that anything was wrong. No, the ball was in his court. If he didn't do it beforehand, maybe he'd explain at the theatre. Not that she wanted to go there. Her face burned just thinking about it.

None of her friends had messaged to ask how the date had gone, but why would they, this early in the day? They were probably giving her some privacy. She didn't altogether feel like telling anyone that she'd been stood up. Not yet. She couldn't face the sympathy.

'Rrrerrfff?' The dog put his paws on the edge of the bed.

'You're right,' she said. 'Enough of feeling sorry for myself. I'm going for a run to clear the cobwebs. Coming?'

'Rrrerrfff!'

***

They returned an hour later, having run along the river path and back. Fi had kept her music turned high, stamping out her self-pity to the rhythm, stamping out her anger. The dog ran beside her, pausing occasionally to sniff out the territory, and once, for a little longer, under one of the bridges.

Fi checked her phone, then put it face down on the galley table and went for a shower. When she returned there was a missed call from Dylan, one from the high school, another from an unidentified caller, and eleven messages: eight from Dylan, one from Nerys and two from Jade. None from Andy.

'What on earth?'

Before she could do anything, the phone rang. Jade.

'Have you heard?' she said, her voice breathless. 'Oh. Um, sorry, you're probably… I mean, did I wake you?'

'Heard what?' said Fi. 'And no, I've just come back from a run.' She tensed. 'It's nothing to do with Dylan, is it?'

'No, no! It's to do with the theatre. Dylan probably knows. Has Andy heard anything?'

'I've no idea. He isn't here.'

There was the tiniest pause. 'I wasn't suggesting… I mean, er, I thought he might have messaged you.'

'Oh. No, he hasn't. It's a long story. I was going to tell you over coffee later.'

'I don't want the grisly details of your date.'

'There aren't any. Look, Dylan's been trying to get

hold of me too. What's going on?'

She heard an intake of breath at the other end of the phone. 'There's been a murder.'

Fi clenched the phone tighter in a trembling hand. 'At the theatre? What? Who? How?' She heard her voice wobble.

'I don't know if it's true, but town gossip says that Jon Angel was found stabbed in a dressing room. Anyway, the police want everyone who was there after the audience left to meet them in the theatre bar at nine thirty. I'm surprised they didn't ring you.'

'I think they did while I was in the shower.' Fi rubbed her eyes.

'So that'll be the actors, us, the front-of-house staff, and I assume the drama students who were helping backstage. That'll be why Dylan rang.'

'Thanks, Jade. Shall I meet you outside your shop in ten minutes? We can go together.'

'Good idea.'

'I'd better go. I must ring Dylan. And I'll have to ring Geraldine and Nerys. I hope one or both of them can cover the boat.'

'You're just ringing them? No one else?'

'I'm not dealing with Annie or Mum till I have to.'

'Er, Fi…'

'See you in ten. Bye.'

***

In the bar, people huddled in groups whispering:

pupils with their teacher, the backstage crew, the front-of-house staff, the Hazeby Players, and Fi and Jade. During their brisk walk from Crystal Dreams Fi had told Jade about the previous evening, including Andy's no-show. Having given Dylan a surreptitious wave, she looked for Andy. He wasn't there, and Fi started to worry. What if he'd been attacked too and hadn't wanted to worry her, and all this time she'd been cursing him?

His understudy, Barty Sheen, was sitting up straight, his expression switching between concerned and smug. He wasn't much of an actor. Tallulah was wringing a handkerchief, her head bowed.

Inspector Falconer stood in front of the small theatre bar, scanning them. He was flanked by two beer pump handles. His eyes found Fi and Jade, then rolled a little.

He held up a hand for silence. 'Thank you for coming so promptly. Firstly, I'll be asking whether anyone saw anything odd before they left the theatre, or had any interaction with Jon Angel after last night's performance. Secondly, I hope to provide enough information for you to decide whether the production continues tonight. The company want to keep going, but I appreciate that not all the supporting people will. As you'll have seen, Mr Andy Hale is not here. This is for unrelated personal reasons and we will speak to him separately.'

The drama teacher jumped to her feet. 'Won't the police close the theatre to do forensics? What if a serial killer's on the loose?'

'We'll have finished forensics by the time rehearsals begin, Miss Brewer. We have no reason to believe that it's a serial killer. Mr Angel was in Miss Levantine's dressing room, sitting at her table, when he was attacked. Why he was there after everyone had left is unknown, which is why we need to ask questions. However, some of Miss Levantine's jewellery is missing. The likelihood is that the culprit was a burglar, who panicked. Mr Angel was in the wrong place at the wrong time, apparently trying on Lady Macb—' A low hiss made him roll his eyes again. 'Trying on Miss Levantine's character's veil.'

Fi leaned towards Jade. 'Jon Angel didn't strike me as someone who'd try on a woman's veil,' she whispered.

'You only met him twice,' Jade whispered back. 'Remind me to tell you about one bloke I dated.'

'Let's not talk about dates—'

'Am I interrupting you, Ms Booker?' asked the inspector. Why did he always make her feel like a naughty schoolgirl?

'Sorry.'

'Perhaps you can tell me what *you* saw.'

'Nothing useful,' said Fi. 'I watched most of the play with Jade, then went to my stall. I was too busy to pick up anything much. Mr Angel came to the Book Barge once. He talked to me yesterday before the play and bought a book, and that's all the contact I had with him. I saw him signing things for people and talking to the mayor, presumably about filming his series in Hazeby. He seems . . . seemed to like the town.'

'Was that why he was at the Book Barge? Because it had film-set potential?'

Fi squirmed a little. 'Yes.'

'I wouldn't have thought you'd want a murder mystery filmed there.'

'It wasn't going to be a murder scene. Nothing was discussed in detail.'

'Mmm.'

'The theatre ghost was upset,' said Tallulah. 'There have been too many infractions on its aura.'

'A ghost didn't stab Mr Angel,' said the inspector. 'And I have no idea how you infract an aura. Perhaps Ms Fitch can enlighten us. For now, I'll split everyone into groups and share you among my team.'

Once the police had gone everyone reassembled in the bar, regrouping in the little huddles they'd started with. Charles stood up, pale but determined. 'It's a cliché, but in my view the show must go on. We've worked too hard for it to fail. But I completely understand if you feel otherwise.'

'We've already discussed it,' said Barty. 'The

company's in. Even Tallulah.'

'Oh quite, daahling,' she said. Her hands shook a little as she pushed a curl from her face. 'It wasn't personal. A nasty little criminal, no doubt, looking for drug money. I trust Inspector – Thingy – to solve it soon. In the meantime, one mustn't disappoint one's fans.'

The rest of the actors nodded, as did the crew. After some consultation, the front-of-house staff joined in.

'I'll have to consult the parents,' said Miss Brewer. 'A few have already said they won't let their children continue.'

A wail went up from the teenagers. Dylan fixed a deadly glare on Fi.

She turned to Jade and lowered her voice. 'I don't buy this... Tallulah had that note and those things happened during rehearsals, then someone was killed in her room, wearing her veil. Surely that means something? I don't believe the inspector thinks it's as random as he makes out. I think we'd be better out of it. And regardless of the death stare, I'm not sure I want Dylan to stay either.'

Jade shook her head. 'I disagree. First, everyone will be watching like a hawk. All the props will be double-checked. I bet the inspector will put someone in undercover. Plus, being mercenary, this will be good for business.'

'Jade!'

'I'm a realist. You can't pretend to be upset over Jon Angel, but Dylan will never speak to you again.'

'He's my son.'

'He's in a crowd of teenagers. Let the school make the call. Then you're not the bad guy.'

Fi folded her arms and studied her feet.

'More to the point,' said Jade, 'will you tell the inspector about Andy? Coming to the boat, then having second thoughts and heading off? He might want to ask Andy what he saw in town.'

'I'm not even sure it was Andy,' said Fi. 'And if he's ill…' The inspector had said that Andy's absence was unconnected. But how did he know? What if Andy had seen or heard something, and was under threat and trying to keep it from Fi? She had to find out.

'All right,' she said. 'We'll stay. Apart from anything else, we must persuade Tallulah to speak to the police. I bet she hasn't.'

Jade turned to the room. 'We're in.'

Fi took her phone from her pocket and stared at it. No messages. She clicked on Andy's icon and typed: *Hope you're OK. Let me know.*

The message was delivered, then read. There was a brief wibble of dots. Then nothing.

CHAPTER 8

'That will be £9.99,' said Jade. 'Would you like a small bag?'

'Oh no, I'll put it on.' The customer paid, then detached the little price sticker from the black ribbon and slipped the four-leaf clover necklace over her head. She took a slow breath and her shoulders relaxed. 'That's better.' She glanced at Jade. 'Could I ask—'

'If you're going to ask what happened at the theatre, I'm afraid that's off-limits,' said Jade. 'The police are investigating.'

'Oh.' The woman frowned. 'But you were at the theatre, weren't you?'

'I had a stall in the foyer and I watched the play. That's the most I can say.'

The woman gave her a look which said, as plainly as words, *I bet you could tell me if you wanted to.* She replaced her purse in her bag and wandered out of the shop.

I should be grateful that people are coming in at all, thought Jade. She had wondered, on the way back from the theatre, whether a distinctly witchy murder might keep people away from her distinctly witchy shop. However, on entering Crystal Dreams, she found Netta dealing with a queue of people clasping various protective items.

'I'm glad you're back,' Netta said. 'I've had no end of enquiries about the best incense to ward off evil spirits.'

'The best way to ward off spirits is to drink them,' said Jade. Netta looked blank. 'Never mind.' Jade thought for a moment, summoning what she could remember of the wisdom of the internet. 'For the best results I would suggest sandalwood or juniper, either as essential oils or in incense form.'

'Could you pass us some?' said a woman with a formidable handbag. 'I don't want to lose my place in the queue.'

'Nor me,' said the young woman behind her, who had a baby strapped to her front.

'I'll bring them to the counter for you to choose, then,' said Jade. She delivered a large selection of essential oils, incense sticks, and a couple of ceramic burners to the counter, then put on the most soothing CD she could find and lit what she hoped was a calming incense stick. 'Netta, drink?'

'Please,' said Netta. Her eyes said *Don't leave me.*

'I'll be two minutes,' said Jade, and disappeared into the back room.

At least the police bit wasn't too bad, she thought, as she dropped teabags into mugs. She had felt her heart rate rise when Inspector Falconer had split the group for questioning, but she and Fi had been assigned to Constable Jeavons, a kind-faced woman slightly younger than Jade, who had taken them to a spare dressing room, asked them both if they were all right, then said, 'I don't suppose either of you saw anything unusual at the theatre last night, did you?'

'Not particularly,' said Jade. 'I mean, we were busy on our stalls before the play and at the interval, and afterwards of course, then we were packing up. In between, we were watching the play.'

'Exactly,' said Constable Jeavons. 'Would you have anything to add, Ms Booker? Nothing unusual at the theatre?'

'No,' said Fi, very casually.

Jade shot her a look. If the constable had known Fi as well as she did, she might have noticed that her face was unnaturally still, in the manner of someone who is scared they'll give something away.

For a moment, she wondered whether Constable Jeavons wasn't the soft touch she seemed but an expert at reading character who would pounce on them and wring out the truth. But the constable made brief notes, asked them when they had arrived and left the theatre, took their names and details, then said, 'I'm terribly sorry to have kept you.'

They were perhaps ten metres down the road before Fi spoke. 'I'm not shielding Andy, if that's what you're thinking. Not really. She didn't ask me about anything except what happened in the theatre.'

'No,' said Jade, 'she didn't.'

'If I thought it was important that Andy stood me up, I'd come forward.'

'Of course you would,' said Jade. 'I'd suggest going for coffee, but we should get back to business.'

'Yes, we should,' said Fi. 'Who knows what Geraldine has got up to in my absence.' She managed a laugh, which rang hollow. 'I'll probably have to work over my lunch break to catch up. Speak soon.'

'Yes, speak soon.' Jade watched Fi hurry away. *She's rattled. And she doesn't want anyone to help.*

The ping of the kettle brought Jade back to reality. *At least I can help Netta with a hot drink.*

She took their steaming mugs into the shop and put one on the counter. 'Here you go. If you can keep going on the till, I'll check the stock and bring more out.' The items she had brought to the counter were already running low. She retrieved the black notebook with silver stars from its drawer and began to tour the shop, making notes. *I'll probably need to place an order later*, she thought, eyeing the gaps in the display. *With express delivery.*

A few minutes later, her list was half a page long. 'I'm popping in the back,' she told Netta. 'Do you want to go for your lunch soon?'

'I'm OK,' said Netta, though the stiffness of her posture suggested otherwise.

'I'll be as quick as I can.' Jade drank some of her cooling tea, then stuck her notebook under her arm and went through to the back of the shop. Once she had realised that the popularity of Crystal Dreams wasn't a flash in the pan, Jade had started to build up reserve stock, and now she had a shelving unit in the corner crammed with boxes and packages. She put her mug by the sink and reopened the notebook. *Silver charms . . . they should be second shelf down on the right—*

'Jade.' It was Netta's voice. '*Jade!*' She sounded panicky.

Jade rolled her eyes. *It's only a queue, for heaven's sake. Everything's got a price on it. It's not difficult.*

'Jade, it's – you've got – a visitor.'

Jade's heart missed a beat. She didn't get visitors. 'Won't be a moment,' she called back. She put the notebook down and smoothed her hair, then pulled up her stripy tights, which had begun to settle into folds at the ankles. She took a deep breath, drew herself up, and opened the door.

Standing by the counter was Inspector Falconer, regarding the queue with an amused eye. He turned as she approached. 'Ah, Ms Fitch. I hope I'm not disturbing you.'

'I was sorting out stock,' said Jade. 'As you can see, we're busy.'

'In that case I won't keep you long. May I have a quick word?'

Jade studied him. His expression was neutral, which was the one she found most worrying.

'It isn't urgent,' he said. 'I was passing, and I thought you might be able to help.' And as he stood, he shifted his weight to his back foot.

This isn't about me. This is something else. For a moment Jade felt a sense of overwhelming relief, then wondered what she could possibly help him with. 'If you don't mind popping into the back room, we can talk there.'

'Thank you,' said the inspector. 'As I said, this won't take long.'

There were two chairs at the little table in the back room now, one for her and one for Netta. They sat down. 'What can I do for you, Inspector?' Jade asked.

Inspector Falconer didn't reply for a few moments. 'I'm sorry,' he said, eventually. 'I was waiting for you to add a smart remark of some kind.'

Jade raised her eyebrows. 'It's not the right sort of day for that, is it?'

The inspector considered. 'Perhaps not. Anyway, I'll get to the point. Your friend, Ms Booker.'

Jade's shoulders tensed and she made a deliberate effort to relax. 'What about her?'

The inspector interlaced his fingers on the table. 'I happened to be enjoying a quiet drink the other night in a local pub. Ms Booker was there, having dinner. I would have wished her goodnight when I left, but she seemed . . . preoccupied. I wonder if you could tell me whether she's currently dating anyone.' His gaze didn't waver.

What's this about? Is it professional, or personal? 'Shouldn't you ask Fi that?'

'Well, I could.' The corner of his mouth twitched. 'But I thought it would be easier to ask you.'

'If she's seeing somebody,' said Jade, 'and I'm not saying that she is, it hasn't been going on for long. But it's Fi's business, not mine.'

'Mmm.' Inspector Falconer rose slowly and straightened his tie. 'I'll leave you to get on.' He opened the door and Jade followed him back into the shop. 'Thank you for your time,' he said over his shoulder as he left.

'That was quick,' said Netta.

'Yes.' Jade glanced outside, but the inspector was already gone. 'Sorry, I'll get that stock organised. I won't be long.' She hurried into the back of the shop, glad to be away from Netta and the customers.

I'll feel better once I'm doing something, she thought, opening boxes and laying out pendants, knick-knacks and key rings. But she didn't. *Maybe it's shock. A delayed reaction to what happened this morning.* Deep down, though, she knew that wasn't it. *Snap out of it*, she told herself. *You've got a shop to run and poor Netta needs a break.*

But when she returned to the shop, carrying a tray laden with spoils, Netta gave her a significant look and jerked her head at the queue.

Don't tell me the inspector wants a good-luck charm. Then Jade followed Netta's gaze to the back of the queue and saw Elsa. She had a baker-boy cap pulled down to her eyebrows and a scarf up to her chin, but it was definitely her. And she had the energy of a coiled spring.

Jade moved towards her. 'Hello.'

Elsa started, then smiled a bright, false smile. 'Sorry, I was miles away,' she said. 'I don't suppose I could jump the queue, could I? It's just that I ought to be at rehearsal soon.' Her voice was brisk and light, but her eyes were wider than usual.

'Why don't you pop into the back with me and we'll sort something out.' Elsa followed Jade into the back room and waited while Jade closed the door.

'Sorry about the mess,' said Jade, waving a hand at the boxes and packing piled on the small table. 'It's usually staff only.' *Although judging by today, maybe*

I should make more of an effort in here and put out a slate for advice and counselling. 'Do sit down.'

Elsa dropped into a chair and put her head in her hands. She was holding a rabbit's-foot key ring. 'I'm sorry,' she said, through her fingers. 'I did come in to buy something.' She raised her head and looked at the rabbit's foot, her lip trembling. 'It worked for Tallulah, so it's worth a try, isn't it?'

Jade sat opposite her. 'The police don't think it's a serial killer, Elsa. They said so this morning.'

'It isn't that,' said Elsa. 'After we were let out of the theatre, I had a call. It was that inspector, asking me to come in. They said they'd heard from a witness that I'd handled the dagger. The dagger that killed Jon Angel.' An odd, half-strangled sound came out of her. 'They took my fingerprints.'

'They've probably taken a few people's fingerprints,' soothed Jade.

'But I *did* handle the dagger,' said Elsa. 'I was in the wings with Andy when he was about to go back on. I picked it up from the prop table and handed it to him.' Her eyebrows drew together in a scowl. 'I wish I knew who told the police.'

'Isn't it good that they did?' said Jade. 'I mean, what you just told me explains why your fingerprints would be there.'

'It's not that,' said Elsa. She bit her lip. 'I made a joke.' Her voice cracked. 'I winked at Andy and said,

"Make sure you do a good job. Finish him off good and proper."'

She gasped. 'They'll think the worst, won't they? They didn't mention it, but they know! It couldn't have been me: Charles and I said goodbye to Jon at the theatre and went straight home. But what if they don't believe me?' She stared at Jade, her eyes wild, with smudges of make-up beneath. 'What if they decide I wanted revenge on Tallulah for taking the role of Lady Macbeth away from me?' She grabbed Jade's wrist. 'You have to help me. You have to find out who killed Jon Angel, by fair means or foul, and clear my name!'

Jade freed herself gently. 'Elsa, I'm sure the police know what they're doing.'

'But what if they don't?' wailed Elsa, and dissolved into sobs.

Jade fetched the kitchen roll and put it on the table in front of Elsa. *Well*, she thought. And as she waited for Elsa to calm herself, her mind raced.

CHAPTER 9

Nerys and Geraldine insisted that Fi take the dog for a walk after lunch, on the grounds that the dog needed it even if Fi didn't. She took him the same way as they'd run earlier, her thoughts churning.

Why isn't Andy talking to me? I shouldn't let Dylan stay at the theatre... Someone's after Tallulah . . . or was it Jon they wanted dead? The murderer must be someone from his own film crew... I'll text Charles and ask if I can pop to the theatre early to see Dylan.

Feeling better, Fi paid more attention to her surroundings. The dog wanted to investigate under the bridge and she checked for anything that might hurt him, but the space was bare. A small discoloured patch of concrete suggested a fire had been lit. The dog sniffed at it and woofed softly.

'Come on,' said Fi. 'I have to talk Geraldine into

staying when Nerys leaves.'

The dog leaned against her leg and gazed up with a pleading look.

'I'm not carrying you,' she said, crouching to ruffle his ears. 'Come home and you can have a biscuit.'

He wagged his tail and turned for home, pulling on the lead.

'Ha!' said Fi. 'Just like Dylan.'

She arrived at the theatre a little after three. She had popped into Crystal Dreams first to tell Jade what she'd decided to do, but Jade was up to her ears in customers, so Fi texted to say she'd pop in later. Various emotions were competing inside her: pleasure that Jade was doing so well, concern that Jade and Netta would collapse, a tiny bit of jealousy that magic charms sold better than books, and an urge to help, even if she had no clue how. If nothing else, she'd go back and make them both a cup of tea once she'd put her mind at rest about Dylan.

Her phone vibrated with a message from Jade: *Need to talk.* Did that mean she had news for Fi, or that Fi ought to talk to her about Andy? Probably the latter, and she was probably right.

Fi entered the narrow alley beside the theatre with a shiver. It was cleaner than usual. Presumably the police had removed anything of interest as soon as the murder was discovered.

I wish I'd brought the dog, thought Fi. *It's*

probably bad luck, though. Tallulah would make me go outside and spit or something.

She opened the stage door to find a scowling police constable sitting on a folding chair.

'Name?' he said, pen poised over a clipboard. 'ID?'

'Fi Booker.' She dug out her driving licence. 'Charles said I could visit.'

The constable ticked off her name on the sheet, jerked his head to indicate she could enter, slumped back in his chair, folded his arms, blew out his cheeks and stared into the middle distance. He looked as if someone had stolen his ball and refused to give it back.

Backstage was dark, dusty and drab, with scenery and props waiting to be moved, ropes coiled neatly on the floor as they would be on a boat, ready for the moment they'd be needed, and control panels for lighting and sound on consoles by the walls.

Through a heavy curtain she could hear someone declaiming, being interrupted, then starting again. On the far side she could make out actors waiting to go on stage. The three witches were sitting cross-legged on the floor next to their cauldron, staring at a phone and whispering. What were they doing?

When Fi found the students, there weren't as many as there had been that morning. Presumably not all the parents had agreed to their children staying on.

The students were being lectured by one of the professional crew. He was pointing upwards, then at various pulleys. The teenagers took notes on their phones. She looked where the man was pointing. The lighting gantry seemed a very long way up. She shuddered.

Dylan was the most focused she'd ever seen him when not playing a video game, happily comparing notes with the girl next to him. By some sixth sense he realised his mother was watching, managed to send 'don't embarrass me by coming over' vibes, then turned his attention back to the crew member. So much for worrying about him.

'Hello, Fi,' said Charles, appearing at her side. 'Hope it makes you feel better to know there are police here.'

'Not just PC Charm on the door?'

Charles chuckled, though his face remained grim. 'He's sulking 'cos he can't use his magnifying glass. Two of them are still sniffing round. Your lad's safe.'

'This is an awful business. I wish I'd seen something useful.' Even as the words came out, Fi remembered Andy's odd behaviour – if that had been Andy – and felt a twinge of guilt. 'Did you?'

'No. Elsa and I went straight home.'

'How's Tallulah?'

'Bearing up, daahling.' He smirked. 'Her room's cordoned off. Neither her main light nor her mirror lights are working, anyway. Only the emergency-exit light. It must have been like that when Jon was killed. Gloomy as.'

'Oh, gosh. Is she sharing with Elsa?'

Charles shoved his hands in his pockets. 'At the moment she's using Andy's room. If he comes back while her room's out of action, he'll have to go in with Tom. Tallulah's the bigger star.'

'*If* he comes back? What's wrong with him?'

'Didn't he go to yours?'

'He didn't make it.'

Charles cleared his throat. 'Oh. Well, when I last saw him, he was pretty drunk. Now he's hungover and nursing hurt pride.'

'What?' Fi frowned. 'His acting was brilliant. Even with all the stuff about the murder in the papers, his performance was still praised. And why was he drunk? Were you celebrating a successful opening night?'

'Not as a group. Andy said he had to fetch something before going to yours. If he didn't make it, I'm glad.' Charles hesitated. 'Goodness knows what sort of company he'd have been. He was pretty low.'

'Why?'

'Someone overheard Jon Angel talking to another TV bod. He described Andy's performance as third rate and said Andy was deluded if he thought he had a chance in the profession.'

'But it wasn't third rate.'

Charles shrugged. 'That's what Andy said he heard. I saw him a couple of hours later, weaving his way towards the theatre, drunk as a lord. I thought, *You'll trip over a kerb and break your ankle, mate, the way you're going. You'd better not mess up this production through self-pity.* That's the curse of actors: dramatic about the smallest thing.'

'If Jon Angel said that, it's not small.'

'Then he rang in saying he was too hungover to act. What's he told you?'

'Nothing.' Fi bit her lip and looked around the grey backstage area. 'Charles, have you—'

'Charles, daahling! Coo-eee!' Tallulah's penetrating voice came from beyond the curtain.

'Her Majesty summoneth,' said Charles. He patted Fi on the shoulder as if she were five and strode off.

Dylan came over. 'Thanks for letting me stay, Mum. I'll wash up for a month, I promise.'

'Yeah?' said Fi. 'Bribery will get you everywhere. How many have had to leave?'

'Four. Honestly, Mum, there's cops here and the technicians are checking everything fifteen times. It's cool.' His expression changed. 'Well, it's not cool about that TV guy. Chloe says the place'll be haunted by a proper ghost now, not just the one Tallulah was on about.'

'Chloe, huh?' Fi eyed the students carrying out

their tasks. 'Which one is she again?'

'Muuum!'

'Seriously, Dylan, it's OK to say if you're worried. I am.'

'It's fine, like I said. Cops everywhere.'

'Three.'

'Whatever. Anyway, did you poison Andy so he couldn't come in?'

'No. In the end it was me and the dog.'

Dylan's mouth dropped open. 'He stood you up? He can't do that!'

'I think he'd had a bad review and he wasn't in the right mood.'

'You mean what Jon Angel said? That's, you know, that thing where something gets repeated over and over and comes out different at the end. Everyone thought Andy was great. Apart from Barty, but that's 'cos he wants to play the role.'

'No rumours? No gossip?'

'Meh. A bit, according to the girls. If Andy's such a baby that he stood you up over some gossip, he's not worth it.' Dylan grinned. 'Is there any lasagne left?'

'A bit.'

'Chocolate ganaches?'

'Nope. I ate both of them.'

'Typical. See ya.'

Fi left, making sure PC Charm crossed her name off his list. She walked along the alley, deep in thought, and nearly jumped out of her skin when someone tapped her on the shoulder. She rounded in fury. It was Inspector Falconer.

'Why do you always do that?'

'Sorry!' He held his hands up in surrender. 'I thought you'd heard me calling you in the theatre.'

'I was thinking.'

'I saw you backstage, and—'

'My son's one of the students.'

'I know.'

'Of course you do. I suppose you think I'm a bad mother for letting him stay.'

'Your life would be hell if you didn't,' he said. 'I understand. We're keeping a presence in the theatre, so as long as no witness is holding back any evidence, it should be fine.' His eyes bore into hers, then softened a little. 'Let's get out of this alley.'

On the pavement, he waited till a guided tour passed before speaking again. 'You're friends with Andy Hale, Ms Booker. He was seen in the vicinity of the theatre late last night. Do you know why? Did you see him after the play?'

Fi shook her head. She'd seen a man walk towards the barge, then change direction. It could have been anyone. It could have been one of the other live-aboards going to their boat. Thinking about it, the figure had been shorter than Andy, and had moved like a younger man. She relaxed a little. 'I was meant to, but he messaged to say he couldn't come. I haven't heard from him since. You can check my phone.'

'That's not necessary.'

'Andy wouldn't hurt a fly. If he went back to the theatre it was because he'd forgotten something, or wanted to rehearse, or...' She stared down the alley for inspiration. Its unusual tidiness reminded her of something. 'Actually, under one of the bridges, north of where I'm moored, it looks as if someone has lit a fire recently. Maybe they were sheltering there. Could a rough sleeper, desperate for money, have broken into the theatre then been disturbed, and it was all a terrible accident?'

The inspector took out his notebook and wrote, then snapped it shut. 'Thank you, we'll look into it. I daresay I'll see you later. I hope Mr Hale gets in touch and explains himself.' He gave her a kind smile and turned to go into the theatre. The kind smile was worse than Charles's pat and Dylan's indignation.

Muttering, Fi made for Crystal Dreams. She'd thought a visit to the theatre would help her feel better, but now she felt worse.

No matter how much she tried to convince herself that it was a random attack, no one had said that the theatre had been broken into.

And no matter what she did, Fi couldn't erase the image in her head of someone at Tallulah's table, in the low green glow of emergency lighting, looking to all intents and purposes like a woman who'd received threatening notes, sitting there waiting to be stabbed.

She needed to discuss everything with Jade. Even Andy.

CHAPTER 10

Jade eyed the queue, which was down to three people, and allowed herself a very small sigh of relief. 'Next, please,' she said, and glanced at Netta, who was hanging up the last of the good-luck charms. There had been no chance to order more. There had been little chance to do anything but serve customers and race to replenish stock. Now, though, the pressure was easing. Once these last few customers were dealt with, she would send Netta home for a rest before tonight's stint at the theatre. *Perhaps I can put in that order—*

The shop door opened slowly and Fi peered round it. Despite their friendship, Jade's heart sank. 'Hello,' she said, trying to sound bright and friendly, though in truth she felt like death warmed up.

'Is this a bad time?' said Fi. She certainly appeared to be having a bad time. The frown line between her eyebrows was visible and her mouth looked pinched.

'No, it's fine,' said Jade. 'Netta, would you mind jumping on the till? I'll be as quick as I can.' She considered grabbing her notebook and writing a quick note to suggest an agony-aunt column to the local paper. *If everyone in town is going to confide in me, I may as well get paid for it.*

'Sorry,' said Fi. 'I know you're busy.'

'Let's go in the back.' Jade led the way and flicked the kettle on while Fi sat down. 'What's up?'

'I'm worried about Andy,' Fi said, at once. 'I went to the theatre to check on Dylan and I ended up chatting to Charles...' Piece by piece, she told Jade everything she had heard.

Jade wished she had grabbed the notebook. Given all she'd learnt today, her brain felt as if it could hold no more. 'So Andy was drunk?' she asked.

'That's what Charles said. Apparently Jon Angel was rude about his performance, so he went to drown his sorrows.' She sighed. 'At least it explains why he stood me up. That's probably better than an evening spent listening to Andy alternating between anger and self-pity, which I assume is what I would have got.' She grimaced. 'Maybe I should give up on men and stick to dogs. What with Andy, then Inspector Falconer patronising me at the theatre—'

'Oh, he was there, was he?'

'He would be. This must be the biggest case the police have on their books, surely.'

'What did he have to say?'

'Not much.' Fi made a face which convinced Jade that mentioning the inspector's visit to Crystal Dreams earlier wouldn't be a good idea.

'Oh. Where does Andy drink, if you don't mind me asking?'

'The Swan, usually. Why?'

Jade got up and went to the kettle, which had boiled while Fi was mid-narrative. 'Oh, don't worry about a drink,' said Fi. 'I ought to get back, anyway. I've already been out much longer than I meant. At this rate Nerys and Geraldine will mutiny, and then I don't know what I'll do.' She ran her fingers through her short brown hair.

'They'll be fine,' said Jade. 'You're paying them.'

'True,' said Fi, 'but I don't want to get on the wrong side of them.'

'No, I see that.' Jade recalled Geraldine's secret visit to her shop the other day, when she had watched Netta. What had that been about? But she hadn't had a chance to accost Geraldine, either at the time or later, and now definitely wasn't the time to mention it. 'Why don't you head back to the barge, send those two home, and put your feet up? It's quietened down here, and hopefully it has there, too. Maybe take a nap, even. Then you'll feel fresher for tonight.'

Fi managed a wan smile. 'I can try. Thanks, Jade. Sorry to burden you with my problems.'

'No worries. That's what friends are for.' Fi stood up. 'I assume Andy hasn't contacted you?'

Fi rolled her eyes. 'If he had, I'd have said. I don't know what's going on with him. I hope he hasn't done anything stupid.' She shivered. 'Yeah, dogs are definitely less bother. See you later.' She raised her hand in farewell then left the shop, looking marginally less stressed than she had when she entered it.

Jade rubbed her face and caught Netta's eye.

'No,' said Netta, glaring at her.

'You don't know what I was going to ask you.'

'No, but it's still a no.'

'Netta, you've worked hard today, and it hasn't been easy.' Jade checked her watch. 'If you can mind the shop for the next half hour to forty minutes, I'll pay you double time for that and you can have the evening off.'

Netta stared at her. 'Really?'

'Yes, really. I have an errand to run that can't wait, and with everything that's happened today, I forgot about it till now.'

'Oh. OK.'

'Great. Thank you. I'll be as quick as I can.' Jade collected her bag, put her big swishy coat on, and strode towards the Swan.

***

Though it was not much past four, a few drinkers were already propping up the bar. Among them was

Kevin the ghost-tour man, bending the ear of another drinker in double denim. 'The thing is, most people worry that a murder in the town will put people off visiting,' he said, and took a long pull at his pint. 'But to me, it's a visitor attraction.' His grin was sickening. 'The theatre's on my route anyway, and now I can include it as an extra stop.' He put his pint down and raised his hand as if declaiming to an invisible object. 'The gruesome theatre murder – but who was meant to die?' *What's he supposed to be holding?* thought Jade. *A skull?*

Kevin lowered his hand and picked up his drink. 'I might put another 50p on my prices to reflect the increased value.'

'Oh give over, Kevin,' the barmaid said good-humouredly, as she polished a glass. 'You and your ghosties.' She reached up to put the glass in the overhead rack and caught sight of Jade. 'Oh, hello, dear. What can I get you?'

Given the day she'd had, Jade was itching to ask for a glass of wine. However, she suspected that if she did indulge, she'd end up falling asleep at her stall later. 'Could I have a Diet Coke with ice, please?'

'Coming right up.' The barmaid reached for a half-pint glass, scooped in some ice, and aimed the nozzle of the soft-drinks hose into it. 'Slice of lemon?'

'Yes, lovely.' Jade watched the glass fill. 'I bet you've been busy, what with the play.'

The barmaid considered. 'Not particularly.' She finished filling the glass and put a slice of lemon in with a pair of tongs. 'That'll be a pound seventy-five.'

'Thanks,' said Jade, and paid with her card. 'Must admit, I thought you'd have had the actors in last night. Before whatever happened happened, I mean. After all, this is the nearest pub to the theatre.'

'Maybe,' said the barmaid. 'But if they did go somewhere in a pack, it wasn't here. The only one I remember seeing is Mr Macbeth himself.'

'Oh, Andy Hale, you mean? I bet he was chuffed to get the first night under his belt.'

'Oh yes,' said the barmaid. 'Full of himself, he was. Told me how well it had gone, and said he was at the peak of his powers. "This could be the start of something big, Glenys," he said. "I shouldn't be in here, but I need a bit of Dutch courage. I'm meeting Jon Angel in fifteen minutes. You know, the TV producer."'

'Wow,' said Jade. 'So he only stayed for the one, then?'

'Yeah, he had a whisky and soda and off he went. Pretty ironic, though. He was all excited over his big meeting, and of course nothing will come of it now.' Glenys looked wistful.

'No, I suppose not,' said Jade. 'So Jon Angel didn't come in?'

'Didn't see him,' said Glenys. 'Plus Andy got

through his drink in five minutes then swaggered out like he owned the place.'

'Mmm,' said Jade. She took her drink to a quiet table, mostly to escape from Kevin droning on about ghosts, and spent the next few minutes alternately sipping her drink and shredding a beermat.

Andy said he had a solo meeting with Jon Angel after the play, and no one's seen him since.

Elsa said Charles went straight home with her. Fi said Charles told her that he went straight home. But I saw him outside my shop. If he did go straight home, he went back out.

Was Elsa covering for him when she visited me in the shop? Are they in it together?

Tallulah's dressing room was dark that night. Did the person who stabbed Jon Angel think they were murdering him or Tallulah?

She could feel a headache coming on. She pinched the bridge of her nose then finished her drink, wincing at the rattle of the ice cubes, and put the mutilated remains of the beermat in her pocket.

What should I do? she thought, as she walked back to the shop considerably more slowly than she had set out.

I have to tell Fi. I can't leave her in the dark. And it's probably best to tell her now, not at the theatre. She pulled out her phone and composed a message.

Just left Swan. The barmaid says Andy came in for

one drink last night then left to meet Jon Angel. He seemed positive. We can talk later if you want. Take care, Jade.

She bit her lip and pressed send, then jammed the phone in her pocket and kept walking.

As she reached the door of Crystal Dreams, her phone buzzed. She glanced inside: Netta had seen her. Jade held up the phone and turned her back.

A reply from Fi. *Thanks for checking. Now I'm really worried.*

CHAPTER 11

Dylan messaged to ask if he could get fish and chips with friends rather than come home before the performance. Fi replied *Yes*, glad to be alone for a while. She wondered if he was going with just one friend, Chloe perhaps, and if she'd ever know.

'Let's hope he proves luckier in love than his mother,' she said to the dog, ruffling his ears. She had closed the shop and was sitting on the roof of the barge with a coffee, watching the river glow reddish-gold as the sun set.

The dog snuggled closer. 'I ought to make more effort to find your owner,' she said. 'I should check for notifications on the lost-dog pages.' She picked up her phone and sighed.

'Permission to come aboard, cap'n?'

It was Andy's voice. Fi jumped and dropped the phone. It slid along the deck, only the gunwale stopping it from slipping into the water. When she finally looked down, she gasped.

Even in the dusk, despite a beanie hat pulled as low as it could go, Andy's right eye was badly swollen and bruised deep red.

'What the... Yes, all right.'

He crossed the gangplank. 'Can we go below?' he asked. 'I'm probably persona non grata, but I'd rather be out of the vulgar gaze.'

'There aren't that many people about to gaze, vulgarly or otherwise.'

'Don't you feel safe with me?' He appeared both petulant and worried.

Fi hesitated.

'You can go in and hide your knives first if you're worried.'

'It's not that! It's—'

'Oh, right. You're angry, hurt. I need to—'

'I'm not an acting exercise,' Fi snapped. 'Don't analyse me and work out a response. Just be honest. If you don't want us to date any more, say so.' She looked past him at the people walking by. Most were taking an evening stroll on the bank, others striding more purposefully. A couple paused to peruse the *What's On At The Book Barge During The Festival* sign hammered into the grass next to the towpath.

'OK,' she said. 'Come down. You may as well explain in the warm.'

They descended into the boat and sat awkwardly at opposite ends of the sofa. In the daytime, shoppers sat there to compare books and chat with Fi about their favourite genres. In the evenings, she and Dylan sat there to watch the TV usually concealed behind a screen. The other evening, she'd expected to be cuddled up there with Andy. Now she sat as far from him as she could, arms folded, waiting.

Andy removed the beanie and ran his hand over his face, wincing as his fingers touched the bruised eye.

'I'm sorry I don't have a steak to bring the swelling down,' Fi said.

'Vegeburger?' He attempted a grin and winced again. 'Look, I came to apologise. I couldn't come to supper in this state.' He indicated his eye. 'I felt dazed and stupid and I couldn't think straight. The one thing I didn't want to do was inflict that on you.'

'You could have explained that last night. I'm not exactly Florence Nightingale, but someone with a head injury shouldn't be alone. You could have had concussion.'

'I'm fine.'

Fi decided to give him a chance to confirm what the barmaid had said. 'Was it a drunken brawl outside the pub?' Even as she said it, Fi knew that on a day like today everyone would have heard about that. And the barmaid hadn't said Andy was drunk. Charles had.

'Drunk? Me? Look, I went to the Swan. I had a whisky and soda and left. I had one thing to do at the theatre, then I was going to celebrate with you. But, er, I met this bloke and he smacked me one.' Andy sat back and stared into the middle distance.

'What bloke? Why did he hit you? And where were you when it happened?'

Hope flickered in her heart. Maybe what she'd said to Inspector Falconer was true after all. Andy had come upon a burglar who had punched him to get him out of the way. Maybe the stage door had been left open by accident and the burglar hadn't even needed to break in. They'd entered, gone to the room most likely to have jewellery – Tallulah's – been surprised by the person sitting in semi-darkness and stabbed them out of fear. Later, Charles had seen Andy staggering and reeling because he'd been hit in the face. She closed her eyes. The more she tried to convince herself, the stupider it sounded. Then she realised Andy hadn't answered any of her questions.

She opened her eyes. He was watching her. 'Andy, tell me. Who punched you? Why? And where were you?'

Andy stood up and started to pace. 'You thought my performance was good, didn't you?'

'Very.'

'So did Jon Angel.'

Fi frowned. That was the opposite of what Charles

had said. 'OK. Good. So...'

'He asked me to meet him backstage to discuss some proposals.'

'He asked you directly?'

'No, I got a text. I was on the way to buy wine for you. I can't tell you how thrilled I was.' Joy crossed his face for a moment. 'I went to the Swan for Dutch courage. I thought it might be *Meadows of Murder*. Top actors queue up to get on that, it's so popular. Even if it wasn't that, it had to be something good. I thought, *I'll get a bottle of bubbly to take to Fi's afterwards*. God knows what I said to Glenys at the Swan. I was probably full of myself. I suppose it's only a matter of time till she tells the police...'

'Don't they know? Surely they've interviewed you?'

'I said he'd texted me: I had to. It'll be on his phone, won't it? But I told them I didn't go. Just before I got smacked, I got another text saying he had to leave and we should meet up today instead. I showed them that, too. As far as I can tell, he was murdered much later. By then I was back at my flat, messaging you, Googling concussion and generally feeling sorry for myself. I'd been buzzing, then disappointed, then punched in the eye. I told the police I'd fallen downstairs. They can check where my phone was used, can't they? Triangulate it with masts, or something?'

'I hope so,' said Fi. 'And Jon definitely praised you?'

'Directly, yes. Indirectly, Barty Sheen told me Jon said my performance was rubbish. I was feeling low about that till I got the text, so I guess that was Barty being a stinker as usual. Why? What have you heard?'

'Dylan says everyone thought you were great,' said Fi. 'Except Barty.'

Andy sat beside her. 'Fi, I promise I had nothing to do with Jon's death. Nothing.'

'I believe that,' said Fi. 'What I'm struggling with is why you didn't tell me this, instead of standing me up. I'd have listened. I'd have understood. I'd have come round. And you still haven't said who hit you, or where. Will it be on CCTV?'

Andy stared at his hands.

'Who was it?' Fi repeated.

Andy heaved a sigh and looked up. 'It was Charles, down a quiet lane. So no, I don't think so.'

'Charles?' Fi stared at him. Charles hadn't even hinted at that. 'Why?'

Andy blushed. 'He's suddenly decided that I fancy Elsa and I'm trying to get her to leave him for me. I— That was why I didn't come round. I couldn't face trying to explain that on top of everything else. I thought you'd say there's no smoke without fire. I swear it's not true.'

'So why would Charles think it was?'

'I argued so much about Tallulah taking a part that should have been Elsa's. I took her side against him: I'm still arguing with him over it. Tallulah's performance is good, but nothing new. Elsa would have given it that extra something. But the thing is, Elsa and I have never been more than friends. Ever. She's like a sister. You have to believe me.'

'Why wouldn't I?'

'Last night, you'd have said "no smoke without fire". Now, because Charles said he knew I'd tried it on with her and she'd rejected me.'

'Why would he say that?'

'She was arrested today. Or maybe questioned. I'm not sure, exactly. But he thinks it's my fault.'

Fi bit her lip. How much would Elsa have told anyone besides Jade? What was public knowledge? 'Why would it be your fault?'

'Charles came round to my flat today, allegedly to see if I was fit to go on stage this evening. He said the show's more important than anything, but he'd be keeping an eye on me. He doesn't trust me not to mess with Elsa. He thinks I set things up so she'd hand the dagger to me and it would look as if she'd used it, so suspicion would fall on her. I said, "Charles, you've known me for years. Why would you think I'd hit on Elsa, then kill Jon and frame Elsa for it, when I'm seeing Fi?" He didn't have an answer, but I genuinely have no idea what he's told the police. I'm pretty sure he hasn't said he punched me. I haven't. He's my... I thought he was my mate. I wouldn't get him in trouble. I wish I could be sure he feels the same about me.'

Fi sat back. 'I'll be honest: I don't know what to think about Elsa. I don't believe you could kill anyone. Or frame anyone, even. But the bottom line is that Macbeth's dagger killed Jon.'

'The theatre's weapons are real, but pretty blunt. You could do plenty of damage with one, but everything is choreographed and practised over and over to make sure no one is hurt. We have collapsible knives and swords for early rehearsals and doing demos with kids' drama groups.'

'Who checks props in and out and puts them safely away?'

'The kids who are acting as stagehands do it. The real weapons are meant to be locked up – but what if one of the kids muddled them, and left the wrong one out yesterday? What if someone was mucking about, thinking it was a collapsible dagger, and it was the one I used on stage instead?' Andy put his face in his hands. 'If you don't hate me already, Fi, you will when I admit what feels like the worst thing of all. Not that a man I didn't know is dead. Not that Charles is ready to throw me under the bus. It's that with Jon dead, I've probably lost what chance I had of getting anywhere.'

CHAPTER 12

Jade set off for the theatre at a time she considered good and early – fifteen minutes before the doors opened – but as she walked to the theatre, armed with a card reader and a cash box with plenty of change, she realised that she had underestimated demand. The queue began twenty metres from the theatre, and was growing all the while.

'Oi!' someone called as she walked past the queue and rapped on the door. 'No queue jumping.'

'Don't be daft,' said someone else. 'She's got a stall inside. And I wouldn't cross her,' they added, in a lower voice.

A teenager with long pink hair, wearing a T-shirt which said *BOX OFFICE*, opened the door a fraction and peered at her. 'Oh, it's you,' she said.

'Who were you expecting?' asked Jade.

'TV crew,' said the girl. 'I was told to be on the

lookout for *Wyvernshire Tonight*. They rang Charles and said they'd be down to do a short piece.'

'Gosh.' Jade resolved to keep her eyes peeled and try to get in shot – or better, shoehorn in a mention of her shop. *If only I'd got Netta*, she thought. She toyed with the idea of texting Netta to tempt her with the prospect of being on TV, then dismissed it with regret. A starstruck Netta would be worse than useless, and she needed her in the shop tomorrow, if today's sales were anything to go by. 'I guess I'd better set up then.' The teenager opened the door wider and let her through. The couple at the front of the queue stepped forward hopefully, to be told 'VIPs only.'

She had expected Fi to be there already, pottering, but her table remained covered. *She'll be in the same boat as me*, thought Jade, *got staff to cover earlier and now she's on her own.*

Charles came into the foyer and peered through the door. 'How's it looking, Izzy?'

The teenager opened the door and craned her neck to see outside. 'Busy.'

'Good,' said Charles, and rubbed his hands. 'Have we got many tickets left?'

Izzy shook her head. 'There's one seat at the back left and that's it.'

'Get in!' Charles said, and made a low, punching motion with his left fist. 'Full house.'

'Oh my days,' said Izzy, 'Martin Marsden from *Wyvernshire Tonight* is outside. He's interviewing the queue!'

'Let me see.' Charles almost shouldered her out of the way. 'Should I go out there?'

Izzy considered. 'You should play it cool,' she said, eventually. 'He'll want to talk to you anyway.'

'True.' Charles lingered for a moment, then strutted through the foyer to the door which led to the dressing rooms.

Jade busied herself arranging her table to appear as full as possible. She had meant to bring more stock with her, but she was worried about having nothing left in the shop beyond the two large geodes, which never sold, and some pine incense cones which reminded her of a car air freshener. *I could put in an order*, she thought, and pulled out her phone.

A cough made her look up. Inspector Falconer was standing there, dressed not in his usual suit, but black jeans and a navy polo shirt. *Could be a snooping outfit.* Jade imagined the inspector lurking in the wings or prowling backstage and a little shiver coursed through her. *Like an official ninja.* 'Hello, Inspector,' she said. 'Come to see the play?'

'Working,' said the inspector. He strolled over and sat in Fi's chair. 'No Fi tonight?'

'Not yet,' said Jade. 'There's plenty of time. Most people will go straight to their seats anyway.'

'I suppose so.' He sat informally, his clasped hands loose between his knees. 'Have you had any further insights into what happened last night? Remembered anything, maybe?'

No one was in earshot. Even so, Jade lowered her voice. 'There was one thing—'

Charles walked back into the foyer, looking excited. 'Let's get them in, Izzy,' he said. 'They'll take a while finding their seats, and we want to start on time.'

The inspector raised an eyebrow at Jade.

'It's about to get busy,' murmured Jade. 'I'll try and catch you later, or phone you.'

'Make sure you do,' said the inspector. He stood up and sauntered off, whistling.

Despite what Jade had told Inspector Falconer, plenty of people inspected her wares before entering the auditorium. She considered uncovering Fi's table and attempting to manage both, but as the five-minute call came over the loudspeaker Fi hurried in. 'Sorry I'm late,' she said, slightly breathless. 'Forgot the time.'

'You don't have to apologise to me,' said Jade. 'Just uncover your stuff. You might get a last-minute sale.'

Fi did as she was told, then sat staring into space as people hurried past her.

'Do you know if Andy's coming tonight?' Jade had

to ask the question twice.

'What? Oh, no. No, he isn't.'

'So he's been in touch?'

'Yes.' Fi didn't elaborate, or meet Jade's eyes. Then she turned away to check her stall.

Jade's mind was bursting with questions. *Where has he been? What's he got to say for himself? Is he sorry for standing you up?* 'It's a shame he can't make it,' she ventured. '*Wyvernshire Tonight* are here.'

'Oh, OK.'

The main door swung open and a man in a Burberry raincoat swished in. 'Jerry Wildacre,' he said to Izzy, who looked at him blankly. He waited a moment, then said, 'Fetch your boss, would you? Or tell him Jerry Wildacre is in. That'll do.'

Izzy sloped off. Jerry Wildacre checked his watch, huffed, and shifted from foot to foot.

Charles barrelled through the foyer. 'Mr Wildacre, what an absolute pleasure to see you. Do come this way.'

Izzy returned, full of self-importance. 'Who was that?' Jade asked.

'A theatre critic for a national newspaper,' she said. '*The* theatre critic, Charles said. Not that I know. Anyway, it's good that he's here.' She grimaced. 'Although it's a shame he'll be watching Barty, not Andy.'

Inspector Falconer came back into the foyer. 'Secure the doors, please, Izzy,' he said. 'We've checked everyone's handbags and whatnot, and all areas have been inspected. The play's about to begin.' He glanced at Fi, who met his eyes then looked away and fiddled with a book. He strode to the doors of the auditorium and went in.

'Will you watch tonight?' asked Jade.

'They're full,' said Fi. So she had been paying attention.

'Right. Well, I've got admin to do, so...' Jade pulled out her phone, opened her notebook, and busied herself stocking up. *Perhaps Fi will feel like talking later.*

But she simply said 'Good idea. I'll have some quiet time with my admin too.' Under a half-hearted smile she seemed pensive and tense, even as she sat tapping at her tablet and sighing. Somehow, Jade didn't think it was the accounts that were bothering her.

Then the interval was busy. Besides, Martin Marsden was interviewing Charles, Tallulah and Barty Sheen in a corner of the foyer.

'To be honest,' Charles was saying, 'I thought a murder at the theatre would mean curtains for the production. However, the cast have rallied round, Wyvernshire Police have been very understanding – of course we have cooperated fully – and we have the support of our local community.'

'I hear you've sold out tonight,' said Martin Marsden. 'To what do you attribute the production's success?'

Charles beamed. 'There's no doubt that Tallulah Levantine is a major box-office draw.'

'You're too kind, daaahling,' purred Tallulah.

'It's absolutely true,' said Charles. 'And Barty here has done a wonderful job at short notice.'

Jerry Wildacre strode up and cleared his throat. 'Indeed,' he said, inserting himself between Charles and Tallulah. 'Jerry Wildacre, theatre critic. An excellent production. If the second half is as good as the first – and I'm sure it will be – it'll be an absolute treat.'

'I believe the production has a fairly short run,' said Martin Marsden.

'Yes,' said Charles. 'The play is on until Saturday week, when we make way for a production of *Run for Your Wife*, and we are almost sold out. However, we are planning to film a performance and make it available on a pay-per-view platform.'

'There you have it,' said Martin Marsden, addressing the camera. 'An amateur production hitting both the headlines and the big time. The show must indeed go on. Martin Marsden, *Wyvernshire Tonight*.'

'Cut,' said the cameraman. 'Nice work, Martin.'

'Cheers,' said Martin. 'Bet you're relieved,' he said

to Charles. 'A theatre production is a big undertaking.'

Charles mimed wiping sweat from his brow. 'You're not wrong, Martin. Live theatre is always a gamble – finding a cast that works together, securing the right venue, obtaining funding – and in this case, the gamble has paid off.'

'Is there a possibility of taking it wider?' said Jerry. 'What I've seen so far is very promising.'

'We should talk, Jerry,' said Charles, patting him on the back. 'Let me buy you a drink...' He led Jerry towards the bar.

Tallulah beamed at Jade, extracted the rabbit's foot from her bodice and gave her a little wave with it. 'I can't thank you enough, daahhling.'

Fi stood up. 'I'm sorry if I'm being anti-social,' she said. 'I need to work something through in my head before I can talk about it. I could do with an early night.'

'I can take payments for you, if you like,' said Jade. 'It's a shame to miss the opportunity.'

'Thanks, but don't worry,' said Fi. 'Here comes Nerys to take over for the last hour. We'll catch up tomorrow.' She gave Jade another half-hearted smile and nodded a welcome to Nerys as she hurried out.

At the end of the night Jade stomped home, tired and cranky. She wanted nothing more than fast food and an early night, but the pizza place and the kebab shop had queues out the door and the chippy was closed. The bag with the cash box was making her back ache. She shifted it to the other shoulder and harrumphed.

What's eating Fi? she thought, then corrected herself. *What isn't she telling me?*

She'll confide in you when she's ready.

I hope she's not keeping back something important. Must remember to ring Inspector Falconer in the morning.

She unlocked her flat door and pushed it open, with rather more force than she intended, and it banged against the wall. She huffed and shut it, then went upstairs.

Once she had stowed the cash box under her bed she investigated the tiny icebox in the fridge, hoping that her past self had bought a large pepperoni pizza and forgotten about it. All she found was a third of a pack of frozen peas and a few ice cubes in a tray. She slammed the freezer door and put the kettle on.

Thirty seconds later, she heard knocking on the wall. *Just what I need*, she thought. She switched the TV on and turned it up. Hopefully there'd be something mindless on to shout at. If nothing else, she could watch *Wyvernshire Tonight* when the main news was finished.

Two minutes later, as she was making tea, her doorbell rang. She ignored it and squished the teabag, which split.

'Dammit!' She dropped her spoon, thundered downstairs and wrenched the door open. 'What?'

It was Rick, of course, wearing a Jethro Tull T-shirt and a pair of jogging bottoms. 'Sorry to bother you,' he said, and he did look apologetic. 'I have an early start tomorrow.' His brow furrowed slightly. 'Are you all right? You seem a bit—'

'I'm fine.' Jade was about to add *never better*, but decided that really was stretching it. In fact, she felt rubbish. 'Sorry,' she said, and sighed. 'It's been a long day. It's been several long days.'

'Yes,' said Rick. 'I didn't realise you were doing nights at the theatre too.' He made it sound as if she was working as an usher, or possibly selling ice cream during the intermission.

'Yes,' said Jade. 'It's a good opportunity.'

'I'm sure,' said Rick. 'But you should rest as well.' He eyed her. 'Have you tried meditation?'

Jade regarded him stonily. 'I'm sure you're trying to help, but no thanks. I'll let you get a good night's sleep, in preparation for your French polishing or whatever it is tomorrow. Goodnight.' She shut the door in his face.

Having turned the TV down, Jade made herself a fresh cup of tea and some toast and Marmite. She tried to watch TV, but between eating toast and thinking over the evening, she missed half the programme and woke at two am, sore-eyed and stiff, still clutching a corner of toast.

CHAPTER 13

Having unravelled her thoughts to some extent, Fi went to Jade's first thing and explained what Andy had said, then returned to prepare the boat for her in-laws' arrival. Andy was back on stage but hadn't contacted Fi again, and she hadn't contacted him.

By the end of the following day, Fi felt more relaxed than she had for days. She had told Jade about Andy, her in-laws had visited as planned, having been convinced the murder was almost certainly committed by a disturbed burglar, and over a bottle of wine after a good night's takings at the theatre, she and Jade had agreed that apart from Fi's love life, things seemed to be under control.

On the afternoon of the fourth day of the performance, she and Dylan emerged from the boat to see Kevin the ghost-tour guide walking backwards towards *Coralie,* waving his arms. He was moving at a comfortable pace and a small group of people hurried in his wake, apparently hanging on his every word.

As he neared the barge, Kevin stopped and declaimed, 'And here, ladies and gentlemen, not so long ago—' He saw Fi glaring at him, faltered, then recovered masterfully. 'Not so long ago, that is to say 1789 – which seems like yesterday to an old spook hunter like me, haha – yes, 1789 after the flood, um, a beautiful young woman's body was found as the waters receded. It is said that her spirit can sometimes be seen pacing the banks as she seeks her lost love. If we move a *little* further along, the sensitive will feel the chill in the air where she was found.' He turned to a rapt woman shivering in a home-knitted bobble hat and scarf. '*You* can feel it, can't you, madam? Poor lass. They never found out her name…'

'1789?' breathed a teenage girl in glasses, lifting her phone. She took a photograph of a patch of grass and river bank, then stabbed at the screen. 'I just *know* she was a French aristocrat fleeing the Reign of Terror. I can smell the wig. This is going on Insta.'

Half the audience nodded sagely, while the others sniggered. Kevin's expression suggested constipation, which possibly meant that he was merging his own story and the girl's words into a new tale. Then he started walking again. 'Now, if we continue *this* way…' His voice receded as he led the group away.

'I wish he'd stop trying to include *Coralie* on his

wretched ghost tour,' said Fi. 'No one actually died on the boat. Although if Kevin keeps bringing them here, *he* might.'

'Can't knock a man for trying, Mum,' said Dylan. It was even colder, but he still refused to wear a coat. '*Was* there a flood in 1789? And *is* there a ghost hovering about the towpath?'

'Name me a year when it doesn't flood,' said Fi. 'I've never heard of a ghost at this bit of the river, and how would they know who she was seeking if they didn't know who she was? As for French aristocrats…' She looked at her son, who seemed unconvinced. 'It's not like you to worry over that sort of thing, Dylan.'

'History?'

'Ghosts. What's wrong?'

Dylan shrugged and his backpack slipped. 'S'nothing.'

'It isn't.'

'We're tweaking the last few scenes after Lady M dies. Charles wants to make sure the battle scenes are spot on.'

'That's not it.'

Dylan muttered and blew into his hands.

Fi gave her son a sidelong glance, knowing he'd clam up if she pressed him. Was it to do with Andy? Had Dylan seen or heard something about the fight or Elsa? Or was it that a teenager could have been responsible for the dagger's presence?

'Thing is...' Dylan shivered and hugged himself. 'Thing is, we've helped out backstage loads of times before and everyone's been really friendly. Now they're at each other's throats. *Is* the play cursed? Mum, would you come in and see if you get that vibe too?'

Fi blinked at him. It was unheard of for Dylan to ask her opinion these days. A million fussing words came into her head, but she managed to limit herself to a nonchalant 'OK.'

When they arrived at the theatre, Fi followed Dylan down the alley and through the stage door. She smiled at PC Charm, loitering in plain clothes, who might as well have carried a neon sign saying *Police Officer: Grumpy Edition*, then entered the backstage area.

She watched the crew and actors rehearse the play's ending. There was a purposeful buzz around her. A group of soldiers waited to go on, carrying branches that would turn them into Birnam Wood. In the wings stood Tallulah, with Elsa and the other women. Tallulah gave a shrill, truncated cry and the women began to shriek and wail. Fi could just about hear Seyton declare 'It is the cry of women, my good lord', followed by Macbeth's response. The soldiers moved forward as Tallulah and the women backed away. Light caught on their swords and daggers and she swallowed.

Charles was ambling backstage, tapping awkwardly at his phone, and caught sight of her. He paused for a second, then came up. 'Watching for Dylan, or Andy?' He patted her shoulder with his right hand, still holding his phone.

Fi dropped her gaze and studied his left hand. She found it hard to visualise Charles hitting anyone, but his knuckles were definitely bruised and grazed, even if the injuries weren't new. His face looked fine. If Andy was telling the truth, he hadn't fought back. 'If it helps, the weapons are all painted wood,' said Charles. 'The school insisted and the police did too, though they're saying it's a random burglary that went wrong.'

'Any idea why Jon Angel was here that night?'

'None,' said Charles, frowning. 'He shouldn't have been. I thought he'd gone. The only thing I can think of is that maybe he bribed the cleaner into letting him stay for a bit to get inspiration for his series. I remember he did that sort of thing. I wish he hadn't done it here.' Charles shook his head, then sighed. 'Has Andy talked to you these last couple of days?'

'Not in the last couple,' said Fi. That wasn't a lie.

He let out a breath. 'I wouldn't bother with him if I were you.' He patted her shoulder again and walked off.

As Fi walked towards the stage door, she bumped

into Tallulah. The older woman was wringing her hands and muttering, her face deathly white, her eyes rimmed in black. For the audience the effect would be mesmerising, but up close it was grotesque, the paint and powder emphasising every line.

'Are you all right?' said Fi.

Tallulah blinked, then beamed her beautiful smile. 'Oh yes, daahling! Just rehearsing. "Out, damned spot" . . . such a moving scene, don't you think?'

'You've been fantastic,' said Fi. 'I've sold out of most of the books about you: I have more on order. And I'm looking forward to watching your films. I have to admit I hadn't seen them before.'

Tallulah's smile faltered. 'Oh, don't worry. Two are worth seeing: the rest you needn't bother with. The books . . . are they the same ones? How lovely. If only I didn't think…'

'It isn't because of Jon Angel's murder, if that's what's worrying you,' said Fi. 'Maybe the papers came for that reason at first, but they've returned for the performance.'

'The play's the thing, daahling.'

Fi laughed, but Tallulah still seemed solemn. 'I'm sorry Mr Angel had to die in your room. That must have been—'

Tallulah shuddered. 'Poor man,' she said. 'The theatre ghost was upset: something was inevitable. Charles has kindly let me keep Andy's room, so all's well really. Anyway, you have a bookstall to run. Later, I shall come and see which of *my* books are selling best.' She waved a hand in dismissal.

Fi didn't know what the mood ought to be backstage, particularly when someone had been murdered, but all the same, she could sense what Dylan meant. There was definitely some edginess in the air. She slipped out and returned to the front of the theatre, squeezing through the queue that was already forming.

Jade was in the foyer, removing an oversized Peruvian-patterned woollen coat and hat. 'Where have you been? I thought I saw you and Dylan pass Crystal Dreams ages ago.'

'Backstage,' said Fi. 'Tallulah seems anxious.'

'Someone's probably been whistling or saying The Name.' Jade wiggled her fingers in a sinister manner. 'Anyway, didn't Dylan say half the actors are nervous wrecks before each performance?'

Once the play started, she and Jade went into the auditorium. With no seats free, they stood against the wall. Towards the end, Tallulah's truncated scream came from behind the curtain, followed after the tiniest pause by the shrieks of the other women.

'That gets me every time,' whispered Fi. 'But just now it sounded so real.'

The actor playing Seyton left the stage, then returned to tell Macbeth his wife was dead, his voice husky.

'Come on,' murmured Jade. 'We know what happens next. Back to work.' They went back to their stalls.

Inspector Falconer strode into the foyer, his expression cold. 'Ms Booker, may I have a word?' He drew her into a corner.

'What's happened? It isn't Dylan, is it?'

'Dylan's fine,' said the inspector. 'It's Charles Ilford who isn't.'

'Charles? He's not...'

Inspector Falconer shook his head. 'A pyrotechnic device went off and burnt his hand. Fortunately, he moved in time to avoid serious injury. He's lucky it wasn't a good deal worse.'

'One of the props for the battle scenes?'

'Yes.'

'Why tell me?'

'Because it was in the wrong place.'

'But I don't know anything about the props.'

The inspector ran a hand through his hair. 'The pyrotechnic was in Tallulah's dressing room – that is, the one she's using now. Mr Ilford had gone in to collect a prop she'd left there and—'

'The dressing room that's really Andy's?'

'So you know that. I thought you might.'

'It's not a secret.'

'Mmm. Well, it would have gone off when Tallulah

sat at her table. It could have killed her, at the very least by setting fire to her clothes.'

'But—'

'The point is, Ms Booker, that the last person seen entering the room before Mr Ilford was Mr Hale himself. The man who dislikes Tallulah Levantine enough for the whole cast to know about it. The man who says he got a black eye from falling downstairs on the night of Jon Angel's murder.'

Fi gaped at him.

'I don't know what you know, Ms Booker, but I'm convinced there's something, and I wish to goodness you'd just spit it out. They'll finish the play tonight, then we're sending the kids straight home. If the run continues, it might have to do so without them. For now, I suggest you get your boy and go home. We've taken brief statements from the students, and may follow some up. If that includes Dylan, I'll let you know and someone can interview him in your presence tomorrow. If it helps, I don't think we will. If you haven't heard by nine, you needn't worry.'

Fi swallowed, opened her mouth, then shut it again.

Shaking his head, the inspector went back through the staff door.

Jade came over. 'What was all that about?' she whispered.

'Charles has been hurt,' said Fi. 'They think Andy

did it and it was meant for Tallulah, but... I still don't believe it. We have to sort this out, Jade. People are being hurt. It could have been anyone going into that room to collect the prop.'

Jade rolled her eyes. 'When I came to this town, the worst I thought I'd get caught up in was Wednesday night bingo. You're right, though. We have to do something, and soon.'

CHAPTER 19

Fi's attempts to make an early exit with Dylan were thwarted. She was just one of many parents trying to persuade their teenagers to leave the theatre. They were met with 'In a minute, Mum', 'I've got to say goodbye to Chloe', or 'You don't understand. This is *it*'. Hugs were exchanged, and fond farewells.

'Won't they be seeing each other at school tomorrow?' Jade asked.

Fi rolled her eyes. 'If I've learned anything, it's that you can't hurry a teenager.'

Eventually, Inspector Falconer came into the foyer and ordered everyone off the premises. With much sulking, they complied.

'It's so mean,' said Dylan, as they walked down the street. 'Nothing would happen to us, anyway.'

'Because you're invincible, I suppose,' said Fi.

I remember when I believed that, thought Jade.

How wrong I was.

'Night, Jade,' said Dylan, as they approached Crystal Dreams.

'Jade's coming back to ours for a quick cuppa,' said Fi. 'You can game for a bit if you want.'

'On a school night? What's got into you, Mum?'

'We're talking strategy,' said Fi. 'We may not be able to run our stalls in the theatre any more, so we need to talk tactics.'

'Oh, business,' said Dylan, and loped moodily along.

Back at *Coralie*, Fi made tea and waited while Dylan collected a large glass of milk and an assortment of snacks before retiring to the gaming end of the boat. 'Theatre work's really physical,' he said, carrying a tray with his glass, a bowl of cereal, a peanut butter and jam sandwich and a packet of crisps. He pulled the curtain across, and thirty seconds later doom-laden music began playing.

'Let's sit at the kitchen table,' said Fi. 'Not that Dylan will care what we're talking about, but I'd rather he didn't hear anything if he comes back for more food.'

They made themselves comfortable and Fi placed a packet of chocolate digestives between them. 'Good job I had thinking biscuits in. Now, where do we start?'

Jade studied her. 'You seem to have perked up a

bit.'

Fi looked surprised, then considered. 'Yes, I have. I've been trying to work things out on my own and getting nowhere. Two heads are better than one, and all that.'

'True.' Jade wondered how to say what she had in her mind, and decided to go for it. 'Do you mind if I'm frank with you?'

Fi smiled. 'That depends on what you're about to say.'

'Well…' Jade took a biscuit, just in case. 'From what you've told me and what the inspector said in the theatre, everything points to Andy. So why don't you think it's him?'

Fi took a biscuit and sipped her tea. Jade waited. 'The inspector probably thinks I'm blinded by love,' she said. 'Or lust. But it isn't that. On the face of it, yes, it's plausible. An ambitious actor keen to make his mark is overshadowed by the arrival of a famous co-star he doesn't respect. What would be more natural than trying to get rid of her?'

Jade grinned. 'I'm not sure your counterargument is doing quite what you want it to.'

'Haven't got there yet.' Fi dunked her biscuit and took a bite. 'The problem with that theory is that on the first night the play sold out and everyone loved it. So why would Andy risk killing the goose that lays the golden eggs by killing Tallulah?'

'That's fair,' said Jade. 'But what if Jon Angel wasn't an accidental victim? What if Andy meant to kill him? What if Barty Sheen was telling the truth and Jon Angel *was* rude about Andy's performance? Perhaps Andy asked for feedback from Jon, they met up, and Andy did the deed?'

Fi wrinkled her nose. 'Andy isn't that kind of person. He isn't impulsive or quick to anger. He's the sort of person who, if you offended him, would pretend everything was all right for days, then say something passive-aggressive to let you know that he wasn't pleased with you.'

Jade grimaced. 'He sounds fun.'

'It's not that bad,' said Fi. 'He's easy-going. Not a stabby person.'

Jade ate her biscuit while she considered this. 'Who *is* a stabby person? And who has a motive strong enough to kill someone – never mind if it was the right person or not – then have another go?'

'There's Elsa,' said Fi. 'She's had a leading role taken from her. Maybe she was aiming at Tallulah both times.'

'I suppose.'

'You don't look convinced.'

'I'm thinking it over,' said Jade. 'Elsa's prints were on the dagger, and while she's given a reason for that, it would make perfect sense for her to handle the dagger in sight of the cast, in case her prints were found on it later. She could have asked Tallulah for private acting tips, and when she found a veiled figure in Tallulah's dressing room…'

But something else nagged at her. 'She made a point of visiting me, and I don't think it was to get hold of a rabbit's foot. What if Elsa wanted to make sure someone knew she had an alibi because she went home with Charles?' She drank some more tea. 'What about Charles?'

Fi frowned. 'I don't follow.'

'Neither do I,' said Jade. 'But my gut tells me that something's going on with him.' She remembered the interview in the theatre foyer, when Charles had spoken of the production as a gamble that had paid off. 'I'm thinking aloud, so it may make no sense…'

'OK,' said Fi.

'Charles has run the drama society for years. What if it isn't just Andy who's aiming for the big time? Charles has more at stake if the production fails. He's put both time and money into it.'

'That poster for the play…' said Fi. 'That wasn't knocked up on a home computer.'

'No,' said Jade. 'And I bet Tallulah isn't appearing for minimum wage.'

'But why would Charles want to kill his leading lady?'

'Maybe he didn't,' said Jade. 'Maybe his plan was to cause a sensation and attract publicity.

Alternatively, if Tallulah was put out of action, would he have to pay her? He'd get Elsa back and take it from there.'

'Then why would he blow himself up?' asked Fi.

'Good question. He knows the police are investigating, so it could be a way to divert their suspicion. Yes, he's injured, but nowhere near as badly as Tallulah would have been. Also . . . what are his injuries?'

'He's burnt his hand and arm,' said Fi. 'I heard one of the stagehands talking. Apparently he rushed out of Tallulah's dressing room and screamed for water.'

'If Andy's telling the truth, I bet it's the hand Charles punched him with that's burnt.' Jade took another biscuit with a satisfied nod.

'We can check that,' said Fi. 'Do we tell Inspector Falconer all this?'

'Not yet,' said Jade. 'Not unless we need to know something relating to the case, and maybe not then.' She looked at her watch and drained her tea. 'I should head back before it gets too late. Another busy day tomorrow, no doubt.' She studied Fi. 'Will you be OK here with Dylan?'

'Don't be daft.' Fi finished her drink too. 'I'll be fine. Unless it *is* Elsa and she comes after me because she's jealous of my perfect relationship with Andy.'

'There's a reason why I'm single,' said Jade, 'and it's men. I'll text you if I think of anything. Thanks for the brew.'

Fi saw her off the boat and Jade walked up the cobbled street towards town. At the top, she turned. Fi was a small figure framed in the light of the open doorway. Jade waved and entered the high street. But she didn't go straight home. Instead, she walked to the Swan.

'Hello again,' said Glenys. 'Are we your new local?'

'It's been a long week,' said Jade. 'Just popping in for a quick one.'

'Diet Coke?'

Jade glanced about. The Swan was what she thought of as a codgers' pub, which was why she had been surprised that Andy drank there. Most evening drinkers tended to come in for a pint or two either before or after dinner, so many of the tables were empty. However, in the back corner sat a group in *CREW* T-shirts. And close by, nursing a pint of something, was Rick. She couldn't believe her luck. 'Could you pop a rum in it?'

Glenys winked. 'Now you're talking,' she said. 'Bacardi, Captain Morgan, or Kraken?'

'Kraken,' said Jade. She had no idea what it was like, but the image of a giant many-tentacled sea creature dragging things down seemed appropriate.

She took her drink and marched towards Rick, who looked up at approaching footsteps then smiled at her.

'Mind if I join you?' she asked, and took a seat facing the next table.

'Another busy day?' said Rick.

'It was, rather,' Jade replied. She took a sip of her drink, which was heady and warming. 'How about you?'

'I got an interesting cabinet in today,' said Rick. 'One of those ones with secret compartments. It's in shocking condition, though. I'll have to strip it back completely, not to mention replace most of the brasswork…'

Jade made appreciative noises every so often while listening to the conversation at the next table. One of the stagehands had seen her approach, and now said 'Walls have ears.'

Jade raised her eyebrows. 'I'm not listening in, if that's what you think. I'm having a drink with my next-door neighbour.'

'Fair enough,' said another man. 'We're just gossiping, anyway. Letting off steam. Nothing in it.' They drank in silence for a couple of minutes. Then one asked, 'So who's the eventual winner?'

'Hard to say,' said a deep-voiced man with wiry grey hair and impressive sideburns. 'I reckon Tallulah. Rave reviews, which I reckon will lead to a – what do you call it? – a late-career renaissance.'

'Fancy,' said a slightly younger man with suspiciously black hair. 'I'd say Andy. For one thing,

Tallulah is lucky she hasn't got killed – yet. Andy's never had this kind of exposure before and the controversy won't hurt one bit. Adds to the frisson of danger, if you ask me. Bet you he won't be working for the Equity minimum on his next job.'

A white-haired man who looked too frail to move scenery had a coughing fit, which he drowned with his pint. 'You two may have all the big words,' he said, 'but you're missing someone who's flying under the radar.'

'Who's that, then?' asked Sideburns.

'Charles, of course. He's the one who stands to rake it in from the production. Yes, Tallulah's on a ridiculous wage, but what you don't know is that she lent Charles a stack of money to put the play on in the first place. Hardly any risk to him, and who gets the box office when the theatre have taken their share? Charles does. Who'll collect the money when the play gets streamed? Charles will. Who'll be seen as a safe pair of hands – no, a dynamite pair of hands – that can be trusted with a professional production? You don't need three guesses, do you.'

'Hadn't thought of it that way,' said Sideburns. 'You're smarter than you look, Terry.'

'Thank you,' said Terry, with dignity. 'Same again for me, please.'

Muttering under his breath, Sideburns got up and went to the bar, feeling for his wallet.

Jade drained her glass and tuned in to Rick. 'And the marquetry is delicate,' he was saying. 'Very fragile. It requires careful handling.'

'I imagine it does,' said Jade, and faked a yawn. 'I should probably call it a night. Back in the shop tomorrow.'

'I'll walk you back.' Rick finished the last inch of his pint. 'Shall we?'

Coming from the stuffy warmth of the pub, the cool October air was a shock. They walked silently to Crystal Dreams. 'Good night, Jade,' said Rick.

'Night.' Jade let herself in, not to the flat, but the shop. She grabbed her notebook, made sure all was secure and headed upstairs. She made a cup of tea and got comfortable in bed, then opened her notebook and began to write, covering page after page with thoughts and speculations.

CHAPTER 15

The morning started with a flurry of texts, messages and emails.

Fi's mother: *I thought you said everything was under control. Weren't you going out with an actor last year? He's not involved, is he? Ring me.*

Annie: *I thought you said Dylan was safe? Ring me.*

The school:
Dear Ms Booker,
The drama students will not be assisting at the theatre today. However, the police may give permission for them to return tomorrow. Please email immediately to confirm your consent to your child taking part. If you do, you will be required to attend

with your child on the afternoon of the performance to sign a form.

Please see attached our policy for school activities and our insurance information.

Yours sincerely,
Miss K Brewer, Head of Performing Arts.

Angel Productions:
Hi Fi,

I hope it's all right to be informal. I'm Demi, associate producer at Angel Productions. I was with Jon when we visited you a week or so ago, and I'm taking forward his existing and planned projects.

Before the unfortunate incident, he told me that you'd confirmed your interest in his proposal, so I'd like to pop round and discuss things. Is 2 pm OK? I see you'll be closed, as Hazeby Writers' Group are doing readings on the deck of the Book Barge, so I thought it might be a good time for an informal chat. Need to strike while the iron's hot. Let me know.

Regards,
Demi Dexter

Fi sat in the galley for a few minutes, gazing at an old photograph on the wall of Dylan in his first school play, then emailed Miss Brewer to say yes. She rang her mother and mother-in-law and reassured them with words she wasn't sure she believed herself. Then she reread the last email.

Strike while the iron's hot? Unfortunate incident? Demi's boss, her colleague, had been stabbed to death, and that was all she could say? Fi was tempted to say no, but... She looked at the photograph of Dylan again. It wouldn't hurt to find out what Angel Productions wanted, but she wasn't going to let some heartless TV producer make her miss the Writers' Group performance.

I'm closing at 1, she replied. *Come at 1.15.*

A reply came by return. *That's fine. I'll bring lattes.*

***

At quarter past one on the dot, a petite woman in her forties appeared at the top of the Book Barge steps with a young man towering over her shoulder. 'Hi Fi, is it OK to come in?' she called. 'I've brought Ethan too.'

'Of course.'

'We've brought lattes,' she said as they descended. 'Well, the closest the place called Betsy's does to a latte, and some Danishes. Oh I'm sorry, we only brought them for three. I didn't realise your assistant would be here.' The 'we' turned out to be Ethan, gingerly balancing a cardboard drinks-container tray and a paper bag as he came down the steep steps behind Demi.

'Don't mind me,' said Nerys, shrugging herself

into her coat. 'It is what it is. I was going into town anyway.' She nudged Fi. 'It's the lady with the phone the size of her head,' she whispered. 'I didn't expect it to be her. Goes to show size isn't important.' She sniggered. Louder, she said, 'I'll be back later to help with the chairs and the portable heater, Fi. Hope that Roger can set up the PA, I haven't a Scooby. Have fun.' Then she approached Demi, who was standing near the door. 'If Fi says yes, can I be an extra?'

'Never say never,' said Demi. Nerys beamed at her and left.

Fi shook hands and took them into the galley. It was hard to decide where to sit. The living quarters felt too domestic, but the dining table made her feel less on display and more in control.

'I'm really sorry about Jon,' she said. 'You must be devastated. I'll be honest, I was surprised to hear from you. I'd forgotten all about it, and also—'

'It's heartless?' Demi's features were just on the sad side of blank as she handed Fi a coffee. 'Yeah, it might seem that way. But it's what he would have wanted.'

'It is,' said Ethan, offering the bag of Danish pastries.

Demi raised her eyebrows. 'You're an intern, Ethan. You'd known him a total of one month.'

'He was a dedicated professional.'

'That's true.' Demi sipped her coffee and tapped

on the screen of Ethan's tablet to indicate that he should take notes. 'It's like this, Fi. The *Meadows of Murder* franchise was Jon's brainchild and it's a prime-time phenomenon. That's not to be sniffed at, with all the streaming available nowadays. The channel broadcasting it makes a fortune from selling advertising slots, even during the repeats. We've sold the foreign-language rights to six different countries, so it makes Angel Productions and the scriptwriters and core cast a fortune, too. Actors beg to be on the show, never mind if they'll be dead before the first ad break.'

'I know,' said Fi, her knowledge mainly based on what Nerys had said. 'But the timing…'

'The last thing Jon would want is for us to stop out of misguided sentiment,' said Demi. 'We've got the last episode of the next series to finish filming this week – we stopped for a few days out of respect, of course – but we need to get it in the can. It sounds heartless, but trust me, Jon would have been the first to say that his murder is about the best publicity *Meadows of Murder* could get. That's showbiz for you. Tears are for in private.' She turned down the corners of her mouth and opened her eyes wide. They didn't look as if they'd been moistened by a tear for a good thirty years.

'I'm glad I'm in books,' said Fi. *And I thought the corporate world was cut-throat. Is this really an industry I want Dylan to enter?*

'We'll be doing a special in Jon's memory,' said Demi. 'If it makes you feel better, a proportion of the profits will go to charity.'

'How much? Which one?'

'TBC. What do you reckon, Fi? We'd pay you, of course, and you'd get publicity.'

'I don't want to profit from a murder.'

'Awooga, awooga! Overthinking alert!' Demi gave a little chuckle. 'It'll be months before it's broadcast.' She saw the picture of Dylan. 'Is that your son in a school play?'

'Yes,' said Fi. 'He's nearly fifteen now and working at the theatre. He was upset by the murder. He's the age when kids don't let on, but he was.'

'But he's still going back each day?'

'He wants a career in the dramatic arts and he's supporting his friends.'

'There you go. A trooper, just like Jon.'

'And supportive too,' said Ethan. 'Ow!' He bent down and rubbed his leg.

Demi smiled at Fi. 'Think how our fee would help with university or drama school in a couple of years.'

'Look, I'm not signing anything today,' said Fi. 'It seems mercenary to me, but my son would never forgive me if I didn't find out what you were planning and how it would work.'

'OK, let's do a tour of your boat. May I take

photos?' Demi stood up and raised her phone.

'Not in the private quarters,' said Fi. 'In the main part of the boat and on deck, yes.'

Demi pouted. 'It's too small to film in this bit. I just wanted some pictures for potential sets.'

'No.'

'Oh, all right.' She walked into the main part of the boat as if she owned it and started clicking and pointing. 'We'd need a duplicate set, because we couldn't get every angle inside a space this claustrophobic. But from Jon's notes... Notes, Ethan, where are the notes?' Ethan tapped on his tablet and shoved it under her nose. 'The character's an antiquarian bookseller who lives on an old barge. Are many of these books antique?'

'No.'

'But they could be. Anyway, his expertise helps our inspector solve the case through arcane texts and secret codes hidden in old tomes.' Demi picked up a brand-new hardback of one of the latest fantasy bestsellers, which had an embossed dragon on the front. 'Like this.'

When Jon suggested it, I was keen, thought Fi. *If he hadn't been murdered, I'd still be keen. But now I feel like a parasite.* She tried to remember what she knew of Jon's private life. The papers had been vague. Four ex-wives, and an adult son who'd said that his father would be missed. 'How will Jon's son feel about it?'

Demi's smile didn't move. 'He'll be delighted, I'm sure. We'd need you closed for a month while we film. You'd get a sum for loss of earnings, plus a hiring fee and incidental expenses, and of course we'd put you up in a hotel. You'd have free publicity and I bet we could get your son in as an extra at the very least. I'm not sure how we'd get your assistant in, but maybe your son could be the expert's grandson. We could even give him some lines so he can get an Equity card. Jon liked to foster talent, as long as it added value.'

Corporate speak, thought Fi, shuddering, then noticed Ethan wrinkling his nose. He didn't give the impression of someone who'd enjoyed his talent being fostered. Perhaps the lack of grief meant Jon Angel wasn't popular with his team. It was one thing to want a profitable production, something else if you demanded value for money from your team but didn't support them. Perhaps the son wasn't too upset to speak to the press. Maybe he had nothing to say.

'Can you put something concrete and a proper quotation in an email?' said Fi. 'I'll talk to my accountant and think it over. By the way, I assume you've seen the local production of *Macbeth*? There are excellent actors in that. Talent that *you* could foster, instead of Jon.'

Demi gave a dainty shrug. 'Tallulah's under

consideration, of course, though we'd have to get moving before people forget who she is again. There's Andy Hale, too. He's great: I'm just not sure how Jon would feel about using him. Ethan, go up top and take photos, please.'

Fi tensed. She hadn't looked at the news for hours. Had the police arrested Andy for Jon's murder and Charles's assault? 'Why?'

Demi waited until Ethan had gone. 'You're a good businessperson, Fi, and I respect you,' she said. 'Did you invest in the play?' She didn't wait for an answer. 'Whether you did or not, there's no way that you, or anyone else in this town, could have put in as much as Jon did. Sure, it wasn't West End money, but it's the most lavish amateur production I've ever seen. So I'm not offering anyone from Charles's company anything till Angel Productions gets its investment back.' She gave a grim laugh. 'And then some.'

CHAPTER 16

Jade's mind was full of the murder. Was it Charles? Who else could it be? Serving her customers, normally a pleasure, felt like a distraction from what she should be doing. She wished the queue would order their spell books from someone else, and in the case of alternative remedies, take paracetamol.

Netta was five minutes late coming in to cover lunch, and Jade rolled her eyes as she bustled in, hung up her coat, and advanced to the counter. 'Sorry,' she said, 'I got held up.'

'I figured,' said Jade, then rebuked herself. That was unfair. When she had first taken Netta on, she had fully expected her to be as disengaged and lazy as she had seemed when she worked at Freddy's shop. But Netta wasn't workshy, just shy. 'Apologies,' she said. 'I guess I'm hungry.'

'Happens to us all,' said Netta. 'Are you going out

for lunch? Seeing Fi at the barge?'

'She's got an event on. We're having supper together this evening anyway, before we go to the theatre.' *But I'll spontaneously combust if I don't do something.* She gazed around the shop for inspiration. 'If you want a drink, make yourself one now.'

'Oh, thank you,' said Netta, and went into the back.

Quickly, Jade went to the charms display and stuffed a selection into her bag. *The perfect excuse to visit the theatre, and while I'm there I can check for hazards and booby traps. If Charles thinks he's in the clear, he may try something else.* For perhaps the first time ever, Jade wished she really did have a sixth sense or otherworldly intuition, so that she could sniff out the murderer.

In daylight the theatre looked entirely innocent: a well maintained Victorian building and pillar of the town. Jade tried the door, but it was locked. Then she knocked at the stage door and a police officer opened it halfway. Luckily, it was kindly Constable Jeavons. 'Do you have a reason to be here?' she enquired. 'I'm not supposed to let people in without a reason.'

'Oh yes,' said Jade. She delved into her bag. 'I've brought good-luck charms for the cast. To ward off evil.'

'Oh, that's nice,' said the police officer. 'I'm sure they'll appreciate that. You know which way to go.

They're rehearsing at the moment. No idea why they need to keep practising, it's ever so good.'

Jade entered the auditorium. Andy was on stage talking to himself while other cast members watched from the sidelines. His eye socket resembled a painting of a sunset by an enthusiastic amateur. If what he had told Fi was true, Charles packed quite a punch.

'All right,' Charles called from the front row, and Jade started guiltily. 'Can you give us a bit more nuance?'

Andy spread his hands, palms up. 'What sort of nuance?'

'Oh, you know,' said Charles.

'I don't,' said Andy.

'Take five, go away and think about it. Tallulah, can we look at your solo?'

Has he set something up? Jade coughed, and everyone on stage stared into the darkness. 'Who's there?' said Andy.

'Only me. Jade Fitch, from Crystal Dreams. I've brought you some good-luck charms to protect against evil. The police officer outside said it was fine.'

'Oh, how kind,' said Tallulah, coming forward.

Don't let her get to centre stage. Jade advanced quickly. 'Tallulah, this is for you.' She mounted the steps at the side of the stage, beckoned Tallulah towards her, and hung a four-leaf clover round her neck.

Tallulah frowned. 'But don't I—'

'I know you already have one,' Jade murmured, 'but not everyone does.' She raised her voice. 'Let me tell you its special properties.' She cupped her hand to Tallulah's ear. 'Watch out for Charles,' she whispered. 'I think he's out to get you. Don't tell anyone.'

Tallulah gazed at her, wide-eyed. 'Thank you,' she said quietly. 'I'll be sure to remember.' She moved away.

'Who else would like a charm?' asked Jade, reaching into her bag and holding up a fistful.

'I wouldn't mind,' said Andy. 'I could use a bit of luck.'

You're lucky you've got Fi, thought Jade, but gave him a horseshoe nevertheless. She moved among the cast, and as she hung charms around their necks, looked up and into the wings, but everything seemed tidy and secure. 'I'll see you later this evening in the foyer,' she said. 'Break a leg!'

'Wait!' cried Tallulah. She hurried towards Jade, a canvas tote bag in her hand. 'A little something from me as a thank-you for your support. Well, I'm sure it's from all of us, really.'

She handed the bag to Jade. It was quite heavy. Jade peeked inside and saw a bottle of red wine, curiously shaped. The writing on the label was not in the usual alphabet. 'Oh, thank you! I'll drink to you tonight.'

She left the theatre, slightly reassured. *I've done the best I can, even if it isn't much. Given the money Crystal Dreams is making at the moment, thanks to this crew, a handful of inexpensive charms is the least I can do.* She bought herself a meal deal from Boots on the way back to the shop as a reward for thinking of others.

The afternoon passed more quickly, and when it was time to close Jade's thoughts turned to the mysterious bottle of wine. *Fi will know what it is, I expect, and whether it's good to drink.* She took it out of the bag and looked at it. *Screwtop, and it hasn't been opened. It'll be fine.* She replaced it in the bag, gathered her things, and set off for the barge.

When she reached *Coralie* she crossed the gangplank, entered the wheelhouse, then came down the steps brandishing the bottle of wine. 'I come bearing gifts!' she declared. Then she realised that the person in front of her was not Fi but Geraldine, her pale-green eyes bulging in surprise.

'Hello,' said Jade, lowering the wine. 'I thought Monday was your day.'

'It is,' said Geraldine. 'Fi asked if I'd mind dog-sitting, as the dog's been left alone a lot recently and Dylan is out with his friends.' Her expression indicated exactly what she thought of this idea. 'Of course, I said yes.' She surveyed the shop, though no customers were there and Fi was presumably in the back. 'Could I have a word?'

'Um, yes, if you like.'

Geraldine opened her mouth to speak, but Fi came into the room and she stepped away from Jade as if propelled by a forcefield.

'Hi, Jade,' said Fi. 'I've done prawn linguine. You do eat seafood, don't you?'

'Oh yes,' said Jade. She presented Fi with the bottle. 'I'm not sure this will go, but I thought I'd bring it. Do you know what language that is?'

'All Greek to me,' said Fi, and grinned. 'At least, I think it's Greek.'

'Do you think it'll be OK?'

'I don't see why not,' said Fi. 'Whenever I've been to a Greek restaurant, the wine is nice. This might be a bit full-bodied with prawns, but I'm up for a glass if you are. Geraldine, can you mind the shop for half an hour while Jade and I have a bite to eat? I'll pay you.'

'Yes, of course,' said Geraldine.

Fi went into the living quarters. Jade lingered for a moment, in case Geraldine wanted to say anything, but her mouth was clamped shut. *Whatever*, thought Jade, and went through to the kitchen diner.

Fi fetched two glasses and twisted the cap off the bottle. A faint whine came from the corner of the room. The dog was reclining in his basket, very much at home. Fi sniffed the wine. 'Interesting aroma. Oh well.' She poured them half a glass each.

'Cheers,' said Jade, and they clinked glasses. Jade sipped cautiously. 'I see what you mean about full-bodied. I don't think I could manage more than a couple of these.' She sipped again. 'Actually, once you're used to it, it's not bad.'

Fi tried hers. 'No, it isn't.' She put her glass down and went to the stove, where prawns were sizzling in a pan with garlic. It smelt lovely. 'I'll just check the pasta is done, then we can tuck in.' She glanced at the clock. 'Oh my, is that the time? We'll have to hurry.'

They ate quickly and drained their glasses. 'That was delicious,' said Jade. 'I'm not sure the wine went with it, but it was an interesting pairing.'

'Yes,' said Fi. 'It would have gone better with lamb. Anyway, we should go.' She picked up her bag and they entered the main part of the boat, where Geraldine was standing by the counter looking like a spare part. 'The dog is in my quarters, Geraldine, or you can let him in here. Oh, and there's a bottle of wine open. Do have a glass, if you fancy it. Or two.'

'Thank you,' said Geraldine. 'I hope the evening goes well.' Jade felt her eyes on her back as she followed Fi up the steps.

***

There were no reports of untoward activity at the theatre when they arrived, and Jade got busy arranging her table. *That wine must be strong stuff,* she thought, as she dropped a glowing eyeball which rolled under the table. 'Darn!' She bent to retrieve it and bumped her head. 'Ow!'

Fi looked over. 'Are you all right?'

'I'll be better when Netta arrives,' said Jade. 'I'll take a back seat tonight: I'm more tired than I realised. Burning the candle at both ends.'

'I don't feel quite right either,' said Fi. 'I don't understand. I got those prawns yesterday and they went straight in the fridge as soon as I got home. You don't think…'

'The wine?' said Jade. 'It was unopened. Does wine go off?'

'I doubt it. I mean, people keep bottles for years and years, don't they?'

'I don't,' said Jade. 'But I know what you mean.'

'Was there a date on it? Where did you get it from, the off-licence? It doesn't look like a supermarket bottle.'

'No, Tallulah gave it me when I went to the theatre at lunchtime.' She bit her lip. 'Oh heck. You don't think…'

'Let's stay calm,' said Fi. 'If we were going to die, I imagine it would have happened by now. Luckily we only had half a glass each, but we must find out where that bottle came from.'

'Here comes the cavalry,' said Jade, as Nerys and Netta came through the door together. 'Am I glad to see you two. Can you mind the shop? We need to, um, find someone.' She burped loudly and put a hand over her mouth. 'Excuse me.'

Supporting each other, they walked slowly to the door leading to the dressing rooms. A police officer was on guard but waved them both through. 'I figure you two are harmless,' he said, smiling, and Fi gave Jade a warning glance.

They walked down the corridor until they reached a door with a large gold star on it. Stuck beneath was a piece of A4 paper with *TALLULAH LEVANTINE* written on it. Fi knocked.

'Do come in!' Tallulah called. She sounded carefree, happy. *That'll soon change*, thought Jade.

She stepped into the room. 'Tallulah, that bottle of wine you gave me . . . could you tell me where you got it?'

Tallulah lowered her head and gazed up at Jade. 'I'm afraid I have a confession.'

Jade felt the room spin and put her hand on the nearest surface to study herself. 'Go on.'

'It was a recycled gift,' said Tallulah. 'You see, Elsa gave it to me.'

'Elsa?' Jade's mouth dropped open. *She seemed so upset when she came to my shop.*

'Yes,' said Tallulah. 'But the thing is' – she beckoned them closer – 'I don't drink any more. Terrible for the voice, and the hangovers... I couldn't give it back, and I was at my wits' end as to what to do with it.'

'It may be as well that you gave it to me,' said Jade. 'Don't tell anyone, but I think that bottle of wine was poisoned.'

'Poisoned?' Tallulah put a hand to her heart. 'Oh my.'

'We're not completely sure,' said Fi. 'Luckily, we didn't drink much and we'll get the rest analysed. But be careful, Tallulah. Don't leave your drinks or your food unguarded, and don't accept any gifts.'

'I won't,' quavered Tallulah. 'Thank you for telling me. I'll be so, so careful.'

'Can we make it to the boat?' muttered Jade, as they wobbled down the corridor.

'We'll have to,' said Fi, with determination.

It took them twice as long as usual, with a few stops to retch in a doorway, but finally they half-fell into the boat.

Geraldine was sitting on the sofa reading *Hotel du Lac*. The dog was nowhere to be seen. 'You're back early,' she said.

'Something disagreed with us.' Fi led the way to the living quarters. The plates and cutlery which she had left on the side were drying in the rack, as were the two glasses. The bottle of wine wasn't there. 'Geraldine, what did you do with the wine?' she called. Then she gave Jade a horrified look. 'You didn't drink any, did you?'

'Gosh, no,' said Geraldine. A few seconds later, she appeared in the doorway. 'I was going to treat myself to a glass, but when I opened the bottle...' She made a disgusted face and fanned herself. 'Obviously corked. I don't know how you drank any of it. So I poured the wine away and rinsed the bottle to get rid of the smell, then popped it in the recycling bin.' She patted the cupboard door the bin lived behind. 'And I did the dishes for you. You can thank me another time.' And as Fi and Jade stared at her, she gave them a smug little nod.

CHAPTER 17

Inspector Falconer arrived at the boat as Fi was putting out the *Open* sign.

'Any chance of a chat?' he said. 'Your assistant's here, isn't she?'

'Did you follow her?'

'No, just came along the same path. So, can we go for a short walk? Hello!' He crouched as the dog ran across the gangplank to stand at Fi's side. The dog licked the inspector's hand, gave a soft woof, submitted to an ear fondle and wagged his tail as the inspector stood up. 'Nice chap. Have you got him to ward me off?'

'He's a stray. I've reported him to the police and various other places.'

The inspector held up his hands. 'I'm sure you have. Dog patrol's not my concern.'

'I suppose you think he should go into a rescue

shelter.'

'I'm sure he's happier with you. I would be. I mean, er, books…'

The dog barked, louder this time, and wagged his tail harder than ever.

'See, he agrees. Why don't we take him for a quick walk and you can show me the spot you mentioned.'

'Haven't you looked already?'

'There are lots of bridges and lots of places where people might shelter. And we can chat.'

'Oh, all right. I'll get his lead.'

They made their way towards the bridge where Fi had seen evidence of a fire. The inspector walked at a nice brisk pace, hands deep in the pockets of his brown coat.

'So, Ms Booker,' said the inspector. 'Have you thought about what I said? I don't want to arrest the wrong person.'

'Have you gone through the CCTV in town? That must give you an idea of Andy's movements.'

'Allowing for the ones that some fool had painted over – which isn't necessarily suspicious and was probably done by someone under twenty-five – yes, up to a point. But there isn't much CCTV. We rely on individual businesses rigging up their own to deter burglars. The theatre only has it at the front door, by the ticket office and in the bar.'

'Is that why PC Charm is manning the lane and the

stage door?'

'PC Charm?' The inspector chuckled. 'You mean Hill. Good description. Yes.'

'So, the CCTV?'

'We can track Mr Hale entering and leaving the Swan fit and healthy, then limping home some time later. It's the bit in the middle that's the problem. Then there were the pyrotechnics in his dressing room, which is now Miss Levantine's.'

'When Dylan started helping at the theatre, he told me that people are in and out of those rooms all the time. Didn't anyone say the same to you? It sounds like chaos, though I don't think it is.'

'You're still not answering my question.'

They reached the bridge. It was a bit more litter-filled, but the signs of the fire remained. The dog whined and Fi let him off the lead to root in the undergrowth on the other side. 'I don't have any evidence to give you, Inspector. Andy says he didn't have anything to do with Jon Angel's death, and I believe him. It's a gut feeling. And I can't see him doing anything as horrible as setting up fireworks to hurt someone. He's too sopp – too compassionate.'

'Has he told you that?'

'We haven't spoken since before the second performance. I'm going by what I know of him.'

'But he must have explained the black eye. What did he tell you?'

There was no getting away from a direct question without lying. 'He said Charles hit him.'

'Ah,' said the inspector. 'Now we're getting somewhere. Not that we'll be able to check Mr Ilford's fists. His hands are burnt: one worse than the other. But I'm meeting him at the theatre at eleven.'

'Don't say I told you.' Fi shivered. What would happen if Charles found out? More than a rancid bottle of wine? And there was no point mentioning that until she and Jade found out what had been put in it.

'Do you really think I would?' said the inspector, and looked down. 'What have you found, boy?'

The dog was holding an old, damp orange paperback in his jaws: a copy of *As I Walked Out One Midsummer Morning* by Laurie Lee. He let Fi take it from him, sneezed, then wagged his tail.

'Bless him,' said the inspector.

'Because he's given me a gift?'

'Not the dog. I thought this might be the spot you meant. We'd had reports of an old guy – what they used to call a gentleman of the road – passing through. He'd been doing it for longer than anyone can remember, tramping the whole country, picking up work when he could, making shelters. He turns up every eight years or so. The last time was before you moved to Hazeby. Great reader, they say. Anyway, he was found here the other week near frozen to death.

155

He's in a care home now, under sedation. I'll take that book in case it's his. But in case you're wondering, he's neither burglar nor murderer and he was tucked up in bed by the time Jon Angel died. The official line is that it's a burglary gone wrong, Ms Booker, but it's not. If only it were that simple.'

***

During the mid-morning lull, Fi and Jade made their way to Elsa and Charles's flat.

'I wish I'd done something which made feeling this bad worth it,' said Jade. 'I rang up three thousand pounds on the card machine instead of three this morning. Luckily, Netta spotted it before the customer did.'

'You didn't have to deal with the inspector,' said Fi. 'But yes, me too. I couldn't focus on stock checking and it took me an hour to work out that I'm still waiting for a copy of Tallulah's autobiography. It's been remaindered so long that I deserve a medal for tracking one down, but they promised to get it to me a week ago.'

They continued in silence along the high street, then through a quaint, narrow alleyway to where an old house had been replaced by a small group of modern apartment buildings.

Jade pulled Fi into the shadows. 'Are you sure about this?'

'Andy and I went to dinner at theirs a few times

last year.'

Jade rolled her eyes. 'Not the address! Visiting them. In the theatre, we're in public. In our own places, we have things to protect ourselves with.'

'Paperbacks in my case and lucky charms in yours?'

'Pfft,' said Jade. 'If anyone attacks me, that geode will finally find its purpose in life. We're going into enemy territory.'

'We don't know that,' said Fi. 'But we do know Charles is at the theatre with the inspector. We've told Nerys and Netta we're popping round to give Elsa our support, and we'll make sure Elsa is aware of that. She's unlikely to try anything in the flat, and there are two of us if she does. And we're both taller than her.'

'Humph,' said Jade. 'You should have brought the dog to protect us. I swear he was trying to tell us not to drink that wine. Perhaps he comes from one of the local vineyards and they trained his nose.'

'Maybe.' Fi shook the thought from her head. 'We don't know what was wrong with it, so his nose may be irrelevant. Let's go.'

When Elsa answered the intercom, Fi explained why she and Jade were there.

'Oh!' said Elsa. 'That's kind. I'll buzz you up. I'm in the middle of another crisis, as if one wasn't enough.'

The door to the flat was open when Fi and Jade

arrived on the second floor. Fi could hear the burble of the local radio station and – Andy's voice. He suddenly let out a grunt, then said 'That's about right. Perfect...'

Jade nudged her. 'You go home, Fi. I'll deal with this.'

'Don't be ridiculous.' Fi marched inside.

The bathroom and bedroom doors were open and the rooms unoccupied. In the main, open-plan area, Elsa was leaning on the kitchen worktop, watching Andy as he stared into the frothy gyrations of the washing machine, which was rumbling away with a full load. 'Hi, Elsa. Nice to see you, Andy,' she said in clipped tones.

Andy turned. 'Oh hi, Fi. Jade.' His eye was no longer swollen but now a mustardy yellow, which clashed with his rising blush. He smiled warily. 'The washing machine broke down. Elsa asked me to fix it.'

'It never rains but it pours,' said Elsa. Unmade-up and clearly drained from lack of sleep, she looked vulnerable. 'It felt like the last straw this morning when it broke.' She rubbed her face. 'Charles is rubbish at that sort of thing. You'd think a man in his fifties would love DIY, but not Charles. I might as well have settled for someone my own age. And you know what it would cost to get someone out. Charles said I'd have to do it by hand 'cos the launderette's a rip-off and right now...' She grimaced and pushed a couple of envelopes away from her. 'Thank goodness I remembered Andy's good at this sort of thing. He's a godsend. Take a seat, I've just made coffee. Want one?'

'I'm afraid we can't stay,' said Fi. 'We told Nerys and Netta we'd pop by to see how you are.'

She fell silent, observing how Andy and Elsa behaved towards each other. There was no awkwardness, no sneaky glances or determined efforts to seem indifferent. Andy packed up his toolbox. Elsa poured his coffee and handed it to him as a friend would. He sat next to Fi on the sofa and gave her an awkward smile.

'Thanks for coming round,' said Elsa. 'It's really kind of you, but you needn't worry. I can take care of myself and so can Charles. It's coincidence, or bad luck.' She narrowed her lips and sniffed. 'Jon Angel was murdered by a burglar, and yesterday evening the wrong things were in the wrong place – or Charles was carrying them and won't admit it. He's at a funny age. And he's certainly lost his sense of loyalty. The press are coming every evening to watch us, and who am I? Lady Nineteen-Lines Macduff.'

'Come on, Elsa,' said Andy. 'I'm sure Charles has told everyone about you, and at least you can deliver those lines without hamming it up. Unlike some.' He sniggered, and after a pause, Elsa joined in.

'Oh, daahling,' she mimicked, 'don't you *know* that

this play is cursed?' She rolled her eyes. 'If it is, that's Charles's fault for going against the theatre ghost and casting a has-been over me.'

'I was sorry not to see you in the role,' said Fi.

'Me too. But I shouldn't be so catty. Tallulah's ridiculous, but pitiable too. I felt sorry for her yesterday, so I gave her a bottle of wine Charles had given me. I thought it would cheer her up. I was kind of embarrassed – it looked as if it had come from a dodgy market stall – but she seemed grateful.' She sighed. 'Charles should know by now that I don't like red. If he's trying to butter me up, he's going the wrong way about it. I've no idea what he's playing at, but if he wants to get back in my good books, he'd better stop making stuff up about my mates' – she smiled at Andy – 'and get us out of debt. Otherwise, he'll have to find another leading lady on stage *and* at home, because I'll be gone.'

CHAPTER 18

Though Charles and Elsa's flat was at the back of the apartment building, Jade waited until they were well away from the entrance before speaking. 'So...?'

'Why would Charles get Elsa a bottle of red wine when she doesn't drink it?' said Fi.

Jade shrugged. 'Could be absentmindedness. Or that weird mental block men have about these things. Like when your parents buy you the perfume you loved when you were sixteen.'

'But they live together,' said Fi. 'He must know.'

'You'd think so.' Jade realised that for the first time since they had drunk the ill-fated glasses of wine, she felt reasonably well. She took a deep breath and sighed it out. 'If only Geraldine hadn't decided to play housekeeper.'

'I know,' said Fi. She ran her hands through her hair. 'Do you have time to nip back to the barge?'

Jade grimaced. 'Not really. I asked Netta to come in early as I was feeling rough, and she gets anxious if she's alone in the shop too long.'

'Fair point,' said Fi. 'Nerys is the same. But I wondered if you'd mind looking after that bottle for me. It's probably no use, as Geraldine did such a good job of cleaning it, but it's still evidence and I want to make sure it's out of harm's way.'

'Well, Geraldine's way,' said Jade. 'Yes, of course. Five minutes is fine.'

They strolled back to *Coralie* and Fi took Jade through to the living quarters, calling 'Won't be a moment, Nerys,' as she passed through. She rummaged in the recycling bin and held out the bottle to Jade. 'No point worrying about fingerprints. According to the information we have, half the theatre company have handled it.'

'Tsk, Geraldine,' said Jade, taking it. 'Shouldn't you leave the top off for recycling?' She stowed it in her bag, where the neck poked out in a dissolute manner. 'Right, back to it, I suppose. If I get any bright ideas, I'll be in touch.'

'Me too,' said Fi. 'See you at the theatre. And tonight I'm sticking to water.'

Jade headed back to the shop, pondering the scene they had found at Elsa and Charles's flat. Was Andy popping round to fix the washing machine as innocent as it seemed? Elsa hadn't looked remotely guilty . . .

but Andy had flushed, and been awkward around Fi. *Then again, he should be*, thought Jade. *You can't vanish off the face of the earth when you're dating someone, then turn up tinkering with someone else's appliance. Even if there's nothing in it.*

And if he can't manage to brazen that out, it's highly unlikely he could carry off a murder without cracking.

Jade smiled. They might not have pinned down the murderer yet – though she felt they were getting close – but at least she'd made up her mind about Andy. *Not a murderer, but not good enough for Fi, either.*

She arrived at Crystal Dreams half expecting to find Netta looking like a rabbit caught in headlights, as she often did when things got too much for her. However, when she peeped through the door, Netta was actually chatting with a customer as she served them. *Maybe I could have stopped for a cuppa at Fi's*, she thought, as she pushed open the door.

'Oh, hi Jade,' said Netta. 'Have we got any of the smaller miniature cauldrons in the back? There aren't any on the shelves, and they've sold well at the theatre.'

'We're definitely running low,' said Jade. 'I'll go and see.'

She went through to the back room and flicked the kettle on, then fished the bottle out of her bag, wrapped it in a clear plastic sleeve from a box she hadn't disposed of yet, and put it in the cupboard under the sink. She checked the shelves and went back into the shop holding two small boxes. 'You're in luck,' she said. 'Last two.' She put one on the counter, then unpacked the other cauldron and put it with its older siblings. 'I'll order more in, Netta.'

'Wonderful,' said the customer, a woman with chin-length blonde ringlets, wearing a pair of burnt-orange corduroy dungarees. She paid, stowed the cauldron in her patchwork bag, and left, waving.

'All OK?' said Jade.

'Yes, fine,' said Netta. 'I think I'm getting the hang of it.'

'I think so too.' Jade remembered how flustered Netta had been during her first few shifts, so much so that Jade had been reluctant to leave her unsupervised for more than half an hour in case she had a panic attack or ran out crying. 'You've come a long way, Netta. In fact—' She paused. *Is this a good idea?*

The business is doing so well, she argued back. *You need help.*

But what if... What if a rival shop opens, or people lose interest, or—

Cross that bridge when you come to it. Just ask her.

Jade looked Netta straight in the eye, partly to keep herself on track. 'Netta, it's time we made you a proper employee. When it was an hour here and there, cash in hand was fine. If you're interested, though, I'd like you to work more hours and learn how to do more things.'

Netta gawked at her. 'You want to put me on the books? All my details, and payslips and things?'

'Yes,' said Jade. 'It'll be a learning experience for me, too. I've never had a proper assistant before.'

'Oh,' said Netta. 'Can I think about it?'

'I suppose so.' Jade studied Netta, who was chewing her lower lip in rather a rabbity manner. 'I thought you'd be pleased. Weren't you on the books when you worked for Freddy?'

'No,' said Netta. 'He always paid me cash in hand.'

Jade rolled her eyes. 'Somehow that doesn't surprise me. Why don't you go home and think it over? You've done your hours for today already. Take the afternoon and I'll see you later, at the theatre.'

'OK,' said Netta, unconvinced, and gave Jade another sidelong glance as she hurried out of the shop.

Anyone would think I was making her do unpaid overtime. Jade went into the back room to finish making herself tea, propping the door open in case a customer arrived.

The kettle rumbled back into life and Jade eyed the cupboard under the sink. Before she knew it, the bottle was in her hand. *Must remember to wash my hands thoroughly afterwards.* She put her nose close to the bottle to sniff, then thought better of it. She inspected the screw top. *That was definitely sealed when Tallulah gave it to me. I remember the seal breaking when Fi undid it. Surely it wasn't the prawns...*

The bottle had seemed charming and bohemian when Tallulah handed it to her, but in the shop's back room, beneath the harsh glare of a fluorescent strip light, it was tawdry and grimy. There were spots of something on it – could it be candle wax? Jade scratched a smear on the glass with her fingernail and it came off easily. Then she undid the cap and peered at it. A spot of wax there, too... She looked inside the cap and froze.

A tiny hole.

She turned the cap over. The position of the hole corresponded with the glob of wax. *That's how Charles did it,* she thought. *He made a hole in the cap – with a needle or a syringe, maybe – and got the poison or whatever it was into the bottle. Who was he trying to kill?*

He knew Elsa wouldn't drink it. She'd pass it on to someone. But how could he know she'd give it to Tallulah?

Unless she was in on it... She's got a reason to want Tallulah out of the way.

And we only have Elsa's word for it that the bottle

came from Charles—

'Cooee!'

Jade screwed the top on the bottle and thrust it back under the sink. 'Yes?' she said, hurrying into the shop.

In front of her stood Geraldine. 'Hello, Jade,' she said.

'Oh, hello.' *What's she doing here?* Then Jade remembered Geraldine's furtive question at Fi's barge, and how she had watched Netta in this very shop, concealed in hat and scarf.

She took up position behind the counter, putting more distance between them. 'What can I do for you?'

A little giggle bubbled out of Geraldine. 'Perhaps I should ask you the same question. What can I do for *you*?'

Jade made a conscious effort not to frown. 'I'm not sure I follow.'

'This is a busy shop,' said Geraldine. 'Well, usually. I popped in the other day and it was very busy. That teenager you have – Nessa, is it? – isn't coping. More of a Saturday girl, really. You should send her packing – nicely, of course – and hire someone more suited to the work. Someone with experience.'

Jade held her gaze. 'And that would be...?'

Geraldine gave her an indulgent smile. 'Me.'

CHAPTER 19

Fi and Jade compared notes in the quiet foyer.

'Definitely tampered with,' said Fi, as she peered at Jade's photos. 'Where's the bottle?'

'In a battered old boot,' said Jade. 'It's not smelly, but if anyone roots around in my flat, I doubt they'd rummage in it. What do we do?'

'Tell Inspector Falconer.'

'He'll have a fit when he realises we've been investigating.'

'We're not investigating, we're observing,' said Fi. 'I'll talk to him if you'd rather not. He asked me to help him prove Andy's innocence, and now I can.'

Jade wrinkled her nose. 'I'm not sure the bottle proves a great deal. Elsa may be right. Charles could have got it from someone dodgy who topped it up with something because the contents had evaporated.'

'Through a screw top?'

Jade shrugged. 'Ask me one on spells. But the rest is sound. Maybe it's best if you speak to the inspector alone about what we think has happened, but not mention the bottle, as I'm not sure we can prove anything. That won't look as if we're investigating. Which we are, regardless of what you say.' Jade started rearranging her display. 'Er, what's Geraldine like to work with? Clean and tidy, obviously.'

'Very clean,' said Fi. 'She loves dusting and windows are her speciality, but she has her own idea of tidy. It hurts her that books are organised by genre and alphabetical order instead of colour, shape and size, but she's great at displays and publicity material.'

'As an assistant? With the customers?'

Fi considered. 'Good with the customers, if bossy. As an assistant . . . a bit scratchy, sometimes. I'll be glad when she's back to Mondays only. And as I've said before, don't let her loose on anything digital. She can't follow computer filing conventions at all.'

'Oh yes, those pesky filing conventions.' Jade's smile became a little fixed as she pushed a notebook under a cauldron.

'Why are you asking?'

'She was quite bossy about the bottle. I wondered whether she's always like that.'

'She likes to be right.' Fi grinned.

Jade grinned back. 'Ah, that sort. Shall I get us

something from the bar?'

'Sparkling water, please,' said Fi. 'It'll be a while before I fancy alcohol again.'

After Jade had left, the staff door opened and Inspector Falconer emerged. 'I didn't make you jump for once,' he said.

'And I'm pleased to see you this time,' said Fi.

The inspector's solemn face broke into a wide, surprised smile. It transformed him.

Fi was mesmerised for a second, then recovered herself. 'I thought about what you said earlier,' she said. 'I take a while to process things. And some of the people involved in this are friends.'

'So does that mean you've something else to tell me?'

Fi picked up her handbag. 'Could we go somewhere private?'

'Let's take a walk outside. My officers can manage without me for a while.'

The chilly streets of Hazeby were quiet. The windows of pubs, restaurants and homes glowed warm and inviting. Fi and Inspector Falconer walked in companionable silence towards the little park at the end of the street and sat under a lamp to talk.

Fi took the scrap of paper she'd jotted her thoughts on from her handbag. 'Much of this is hearsay,' she said, 'but you asked me to tell you what I'd noticed, so here goes. Both Tallulah and Jon gave Charles money to invest in the play – a lot of money – and he seems to have spent it. When Jade and I visited Elsa to see if she needed support this morning, what she said suggested that money was tight. What if all the investments and his savings are gone and there's no hope of making enough profit to pay the investors back, let alone Tallulah's fee?'

'Good question.' The inspector had his notebook open and his pencil poised.

'I think Andy challenged him and the row led to their punch-up. Andy and Elsa are good friends. Andy wouldn't like seeing her in debt.' Fi swallowed, and hoped the inspector hadn't noticed. 'I feel awful for saying this, but I think Charles killed Jon Angel, hoping the debt would die with him. Jon Angel's associate producer, Demi Dexter, visited me about some filming he wanted to do on the barge. She knows about Jon's loan to Charles.'

'Ah.' Inspector Falconer scribbled a note. His profile gave little away.

'You must believe Tallulah is under threat too, or you wouldn't be hanging around waiting for someone to make a move.'

He looked at her, his expression still impassive but his eyes troubled. 'No comment.'

'Huh,' said Fi. 'You should be watching Charles, not Andy. Andy had nothing to gain from killing Jon Angel. If Jon didn't rate him, that would be just one more rejection. Actors are used to that. He has nothing to gain from killing Tallulah, either. She's bringing in the critics, who then see him too.'

Inspector Falconer made another squiggle in his notebook. 'Thank you. I'll look into all that.' He cleared his throat and glanced at his watch. 'It'll be the interval soon. I'll go back to the station to check whether our files corroborate what you've said. Nice as it is to sit out under the stars, it's pretty cold. Next time a pub, maybe?' He stood up and made an elaborate bow. 'Let us return to the theatre, milady. Forsooth, one rejoiceth in thy confidences. If one canst, and thou welcometh it, shall one visit thee at the barge later if one hast any, er, updates?' He extended a hand.

'Milady would be delighted,' said Fi, suppressing a giggle. They hurried back, her heart lighter than it had been for a long time. The police spotlight was finally on Charles and therefore off Andy, and Tallulah would be safe.

***

Inspector Falconer arrived at the barge shortly after Fi and Dylan had returned. However, his sparkle had disappeared. Her heart sank a little and her hands tensed. He chatted with Dylan about the video games his own son played. Fi took that to be a suggestion that she let Dylan play one to give them privacy.

'Way to go, Mum!' said Dylan, rushing to the aft

where they kept the games consoles.

'Headphones on, mind. I prefer not to be disturbed by the slaughter of zombies.' She ushered the inspector into the galley, where Dylan wouldn't be able to hear them. 'Coffee? Tea?'

'No thanks, I won't stay.' Inspector Falconer hadn't even removed his coat, and his only sign of friendliness was ruffling the dog on the head. 'Fi, what you told me was really valuable. It all fitted together perfectly.'

'There's a but, isn't there?' said Fi.

'Yes. Charles admitted to hitting Andy. He gave another reason than the one you suggested, but he did hit him.'

I can't face asking the reason, thought Fi, her heart sinking. 'So he's violent, which means he could have killed Jon Angel.'

'But he didn't,' said the inspector. 'He couldn't have. Even if he hadn't had a witness for his alibi, something else proves it. Many left-handed people are fairly ambidextrous, but Charles isn't one of them. Andy called Charles a southpaw and confirmed that Charles punched him with his left hand. Charles can't use a phone right-handed. He can't raise a glass right-handed without spilling it. He can't use a knife right-handed, not with any power. According to the pathologist, Jon Angel was stabbed in the heart from under his ribs by a right-handed person. He was facing his attacker, possibly while sitting in the chair, or possibly he dropped into it as he collapsed. It was either a lucky thrust of the knife, or the murderer knew where to attack. He'd have died very quickly and then, presumably, his murderer dressed him up in the veil.' The disgust on the inspector's face softened as he focused on Fi. 'I'm sorry, but the debt aspect doesn't hold water, either. It was a good theory, but it's wrong. I'm not at liberty to explain any more than that. On the other hand, Charles has given us a good deal of evidence about someone who seems to be lying through his teeth. A good actor, shall we say?'

His face was full of pity. He reached towards Fi's arm. She shrank from his hand, which he pulled back and clasped firmly. 'Take care, Ms Booker,' he said. 'I'd tell you to go away for a few days but you wouldn't listen, would you?'

'No. Thanks for your concern. I'll see you out.'

Fi watched him cross the gangplank then stride along the towpath, hunched in his coat. She leaned against the rail, her head in her hands, and pulled out her phone to text Jade. Before she could, though, the phone rang. She didn't recognise the number.

'Hello?'

'It's Charles. I got your number from the box-office staff.'

Fi's heart missed a beat. Why was he ringing? The inspector had said that he wouldn't tell anyone what she'd said.

'I know ish late, but I wanna tell you shomething,' Charles slurred. 'You gotta stay away from Andy.'

'Why?'

'I don't know what he told you about the black eye, but...' A deep sniff. 'It was me. Ish . . . it's unprofessionalal, especially since I need him on stage, but I lost my rag. He was boasting that he'd be on TV, and Elsha too. He says he meant she'd be with him as an actor, but I know different. I didn't want to tell you, Fi. I thought Andy had broken up with you. But then I heard him talking to Elsa like you were still an item, and Elsa said "but not for long". It's cosh they want to be together.'

'Elsa and Andy are just good friends.'

'I found his shirt mixshed up with Elsha's in the laundry,' said Charles. 'A man's shirt, definitely. Not mine, no.'

'Are you sure it's not Elsa's?' said Fi. 'Lots of women wear men's shirts. I do.'

'How am I supposed to know all her clothes?' Fi rolled her eyes, then heard a sob. 'But I shwear she's washed it about a million times,' said Charles. 'She says she can't get the shtai . . . stains out. How did it get so dirty, eh? And they're always headsh together, bad-mouthing Tallulah. Tallulah, who's making this show a succesh! I'm not giving this show up before the run's over – I won't! But once it is, and probate's through on my gran's eshtate, I'll – I'll—'

'Your gran's estate?' said Fi. 'It's none of my business, but…'

'She got to ninety-eight,' said Charles. 'Ninety-eight. Outlived my mum. Left me a fortune. Top shecret, Fi. Top shecret…' His voice cracked, sobs and gulps breaking up his words. 'I was going to share it with Elsa. Her and me, flashy wedding in the Caribbean, production company, fancy marina apartment, you name it. But now… Once this play's wrapped, Fi, I'm sacking the lot of them and shtarting again. You keep away from Andy Hale. He's not worth the dust under your feet.' The phone went dead.

Fi shivered, cold seeping through to her bones, the only warmth that of the dog as he leaned against her. He barked, a tiny inquisitive woof, and she looked up. A slender figure, wrapped in a coat, was standing on the bank. She gasped. The deck lights were low and the person's hood was up. She couldn't see his face. Andy? But it wasn't his sort of outfit.

'Books?' said a male voice she didn't know.

The dog barked louder.

'We're shut till ten tomorrow,' said Fi, backing towards the wheelhouse. 'W-we don't hold cash on the premises.'

'Oh sorry, no! Don't be scared!' said the man, pushing his hood back. He was young, awkward. 'I was checking if the dog was the one I thought he was.

Books is his name. He's my granddad's dog. I came last week, but you were busy. You're never in when I'm around, and I'm not much cop at phones and Facebook and that.'

Fi felt the dog's tail thump her leg. He showed no sign of moving from her side, but he definitely recognised the man.

'Can you . . . can you come back with proof?' Tears pricked Fi's eyes. 'I have to be sure.'

'Yeah, of course. Grandad can't have him any more and we need time to make a home for him. But I thought you'd like to know you won't be stuck with him much longer. Saturday all right? Six o'clock?'

'Saturday. Six o'clock,' said Fi. She heard her voice crack and clamped her mouth shut.

The young man waved then walked away, taking more of her heart and her confidence with every step.

CHAPTER 20

Jade had just finished a late supper of beans on toast. She was debating whether she could be bothered to wash up a small pan, a plate, and a knife and fork when her mobile rang. *Bit late*, thought Jade. *This had better not be a call about super-fast broadband.*

But the display said *Fi*.

Jade frowned for an instant. *Not like Fi to phone at this time*. That meant it must be important. She pressed *Answer*.

'Is this a bad time?' asked Fi.

'It depends. What's up?'

'Everything.' Fi sounded defeated. 'Are you sure you don't mind talking? I know it's late, but—'

'What's happened?' Jade's mind came up with various possibilities, none good. 'Are you all right? Should I come over?'

'I'm fine,' said Fi. 'I suppose. Feeling a complete

fool.'

Oh no. 'Do you have biscuits? I mean nice biscuits, not healthy ones.'

'I, um…'

Jade got up and checked the kitchenette cupboards. As she had hoped, there was a packet of milk chocolate Hobnobs on a high shelf. 'Right, I'll be down in a few minutes with biscuits.'

'Are you sure?'

'Yes. Put the kettle on.'

***

'Sorry,' said Fi, for perhaps the fifth time. 'I thought about ringing Jenny instead, or maybe Stuart, but even though they're good friends, the thought of having to explain it all…'

'That's OK.' They were sitting at the galley table with a mug of tea each and the biscuits between them.

'I don't know who to believe,' said Fi. 'My heart says Andy didn't do it, but Inspector Falconer seems convinced that Charles couldn't have, and when Charles rang me…' She took her mug in both hands and sipped. 'How could I be so wrong?'

'I've been wrong about men a lot more times than I've been right,' said Jade. 'The easiest way is not to trust any of them.'

Fi's mouth curved in a sad smile. 'Maybe you're right.' She sipped her tea again. 'I'm sorry to drag you over.'

'Hey, you didn't. I came, remember? This is just an excuse to eat biscuits, frankly.'

'Yeah.' Fi reached out and patted Jade's arm. 'I thought we'd cracked it. Inspector Falconer was so impressed with our theory. Then he came back and squashed it, and the worst of it was that he pitied me for sticking up for Andy. I could see it in his face, clear as day. Charles rang, and what he said trampled all over our theory too. But to top it off, some lad called round who thinks the dog is his grandfather's. Books, he's called.'

They heard a gentle thumping from the corner: the dog's tail against his basket.

'Good dog,' said Jade, stroking his head. She sighed. 'So what do we do now? Do we go to the inspector and tell him absolutely everything we know about Andy – including the visit to Jon Angel? Or do we keep quiet and keep digging?'

'Option B,' Fi replied at once. 'I can't face another false dawn with Inspector Falconer. I just—' She set her mug down with a clack. 'Why can't things go right for once?'

'Andy is an idiot,' said Jade. 'I don't know whether he stabbed Jon Angel or booby-trapped Charles, or whether he *is* carrying on with Elsa behind Charles's back. What I do know is that he's an idiot and you're better off without him. You're too good for him.'

'Huh,' said Fi, but she looked a little brighter.

'As for the inspector—'

'Oh don't,' said Fi. 'He's just trying to do his job. It isn't his fault.'

'Mmm,' said Jade. 'I'll let you sleep on that one. But I agree that we should keep digging. Maybe, if we keep going, we'll come out the other side.'

***

Jade walked home. The streets were quiet, apart from the odd snatch of music or laughter as she passed a pub. She considered popping into the Swan and seeing whether she could overhear anything useful, but she wasn't in the mood for Glenys's banter. Plus she didn't want to bump into Rick and run the risk of giving him any ideas. *I'm sure he's a nice enough man*, she thought, though she hadn't really considered it, *but I'm better off alone.*

She let herself into the flat and began to get ready for bed. But even as she put on her pyjamas, thoughts of the case were running through her head.

Charles couldn't have stabbed Jon Angel...

Fi doesn't think Andy did. I don't think I do, either. He doesn't have it in him.

So who's left? Who has a motive? Who's lurking in the shadows?

She closed her eyes, and after a few moments a face swam into her mind. She smiled, and reached for her toothbrush.

But how do I reach that person?

***

'I'm sorry to bother you,' said Jade, the next day. 'It's just that – well, I've managed to lose my lucky stone.' She had rehearsed this line several times on the way over, and now she could say it without even a hint of a smile. 'I've been retracing my steps but I've had no luck so far. Then I remembered visiting you with Fi the other day.'

'Oh yes,' said Elsa. 'I haven't seen it, but that doesn't mean it isn't here. I'm not the world's best housekeeper, as you've probably gathered.'

'You haven't seen my flat,' said Jade. 'Would you mind if I popped in and had a quick check? I can remember where I sat. I won't be more than a couple of minutes.'

'That's fine,' said Elsa. 'It's not like I'm busy.' Jade looked at her properly; she had been so busy concentrating on her own performance that she had talked at Elsa rather than to her. There were shadows under Elsa's eyes, and she was wearing pyjamas at lunchtime.

'Is Charles in?' Jade asked, following Elsa into the flat and making a show of patting the sofa cushions.

Elsa snorted. 'No, he isn't. He came in late last night, absolutely hammered – I heard him crashing around – and never made it to bed. I found him on the sofa this morning. When he did wake up he made himself a black coffee, spent five minutes in the bathroom, then left with barely a word. I don't know what it is.'

I can guess, thought Jade. *But is this true, or are you framing him?*

'I know what he thinks about Andy,' said Elsa. 'That old chestnut's been on his mind for years, but it isn't true. Andy's like my annoying older brother, and he says I'm basically his irritating kid sister. It's different on stage, obviously, but we're actors. Charles is insecure. Of course he is: he's fifteen years older than me.' She shrugged. 'Let's face it, if I'd wanted to I could have gone off with any number of actors over the years. It isn't as if I've stuck with Charles because he's brought me fame and fortune.' She sighed. 'And the one time I think I'm on to something good, he brings Tallulah in and knocks me down to Lady Macduff.'

'That must have hurt.'

'It did. I told myself that it was for the good of the production and good for Charles, but yes, it hurts. I mean, I booked time off work thinking I'd be giving my Lady Macbeth, and… You get used to that sort of thing, though, in this business. Always the bridesmaid.' She smiled a wry smile that didn't reach her eyes.

'I'm sorry,' said Jade. 'Maybe next time…'

'Yeah, right,' Elsa replied. 'The mantra of all am-dram actors.' She huffed out a sigh. 'Anyway, the production has succeeded in spite of everything, and that's got to be good for Charles. He's so bitter sometimes.' She sat down in the armchair. 'Even when he does well, he's not happy. He looks for anything that could threaten it. On the first night of the play we didn't go out and celebrate. We went straight home, because Charles wanted to go over the performance and write notes for the cast.' She laughed, without humour. 'He sat scribbling and seething, apart from when he popped out – to the shop for some chocolate, he said. Then he came back, had a shower and went to bed. He was in a right mood. He's only just admitted he went out to confront Andy and hit him. I didn't know, and I still don't understand why he thinks Andy and I are remotely interested in each other romantically. I was so bored that I spent ages on the phone to my mum, telling her about the play. At least *she's* proud of me. And it's lucky I did ring my mum, because I found out later that that was when – when you-know-what happened. With Jon Angel. So at least the police know it wasn't me.'

'Of course not,' said Jade. *I bet the police have checked the phone records. If Elsa was at home, and Charles too...*

'Are you trying to sense the vibes?' said Elsa. Jade stared at her. 'To find your stone.'

'Oh, um, yes,' said Jade. Reluctantly, she put her

hands to her temples and closed her eyes. 'Wait a minute... Ah, yes.' She reached under the sofa and brought out the small blue stone which she had tucked into her sleeve earlier. 'I thought so.'

'Oh good!' Elsa clapped her hands. 'I'm so glad you found it.' Then her face fell. 'I wish I had a lucky stone.'

'Maybe you have,' said Jade. 'Why don't you pop into the shop sometime and choose one, as a thank-you.' *Perhaps that will make me feel less guilty*, she thought, but the delight on Elsa's face made her feel even worse.

CHAPTER 21

Business at the Book Barge slowed in the afternoon. Once Nerys had left Fi sat at the counter, using the lull before Dylan came home to go through stock records and take her mind off everything else. Every time she remembered the inspector's pitying look and Charles's slurring, sobbing voice, her face burned and she felt sick.

She'd gone for a walk with Jade at lunchtime, and heard what Jade had learnt from Elsa that morning. The police must have checked her mobile usage, but could it be pinpointed that accurately and that quickly, down to an individual address?

Fi sighed. It didn't matter. Inspector Falconer was convinced and he wasn't a fool. Maybe he thought Fi was, though, and he'd been jollying her along, pretending to investigate her suggestions. But he'd seemed open to her ideas at first, only putting on his official manner when he came to tell her she was wrong. At least Fi hadn't dragged Jade's name into things, so the inspector only thought one of them was an idiot.

And now that perfect picture was incomplete again. Fi was sure someone had said something which would supply the vital missing piece, or at least one of them. However, she couldn't pinpoint it, so she'd settled to stock-checking to clear her mind.

So far, it wasn't working.

The additional afternoons that Geraldine had worked while Fi was busy at the theatre had proved problematic. Geraldine had logged new stock deliveries in her own special way while dealing with customers. If Geraldine had been twenty years older, Fi would have wondered if she had been a Cold War code setter and left a hidden message in her database. As she wasn't, it was clearly just annoying chaos. Fi was doomed to cross-referencing emails, delivery notes, receipt copies and half-emptied boxes with her stock records, muttering and despairing all the while.

The dog had climbed into her lap, which didn't help. 'If you could read and talk, we could do this together,' said Fi. 'And you could tell me what you think about last night's visitor.'

'Rrrerrfff?'

'You know which one,' said Fi, ruffling him between the ears. 'The one who called you . . . that weird name.' She couldn't bring herself to say it. There was a name in her own head which would never be used, but until she had to let the dog go she couldn't think of him as anything else.

The dog rested his chin on the delivery notes and stared at the laptop screen, with not much less comprehension than Fi.

'*And* that secondhand book dealer's still giving me excuses about why he hasn't sent Tallulah's autobiography,' Fi grumbled, wading through the most recent emails. 'It'll be so much wasted outlay and opportunity by the time it arrives, at this rate.'

The dog pricked up his ears and looked towards the doorway.

'Hi! It's your favourite TV producer!' Demi waved from the top of the steps, then moved back. 'After you, Miss Levantine. Hope you don't mind, Fi, but I've brought your *Open* sign in. It'll be easier to talk if you don't have customers.'

'How do you know there aren't any here now?' said Fi, putting down a stack of papers and opening the door into the living quarters for the dog to go to his basket. She returned to see Tallulah descend into the boat as if the steps were a golden staircase in a musical spectacular.

'I guessed,' said Demi, following Tallulah in a more normal fashion. 'The town's a bit dead.' She peeped into the aft area of the boat, which was partly hidden by a curtain. 'If you do have any customers, we can ask their opinions.'

'I don't, as it happens,' said Fi. 'But if a customer does arrive, I want them to buy books.' She waited for an answering woof from the dog, but none was forthcoming. He only responded to the word occasionally. Maybe it wasn't his name after all.

Tallulah drifted about, peering at the shelves, picking up items from the sundries table, and standing on tiptoe to peek out of the windows. She seemed less nervous than the previous evening, but still tense. Without the heavy stage make-up, she looked softer and more delicate: her fine, high cheekbones fragile, the scarlet smile uncertain. But her wide thick-lashed eyes, while anxious, were also watchful. Then again, Tallulah had had several near-misses in the theatre, and one man had been murdered and another injured in her dressing room. No wonder she was twitchy; Fi would have been running for the hills. Either Tallulah didn't realise that her leading man was the chief suspect, or she was a true professional determined to see the play through to the end.

'I haven't had a chance to discuss your email fully with my accountant,' said Fi. She had barely mentioned it to Stuart, but Demi didn't need to know that.

'Really?' said Demi, as if an offer of a billion

pounds in gold had been rejected. 'Well, Miss Levantine and I are here to help.'

'Ms Dexter has offered me the starring role in the special,' said Tallulah. 'As a tribute to dear Jon.'

'I discovered Miss Levantine mentored him in the olden— I mean, his early career,' said Demi. 'It seemed the perfect tribute.'

'So I wanted to get a feel for the boat.' Tallulah scanned the space again and turned to Demi. 'It's rather small, daahling.'

Demi smiled her bland smile, then sat on the sofa and began tapping on a tablet.

'I thought the character on the barge was an elderly male antiquarian,' said Fi.

Tallulah's face twitched in a way that suggested her eyebrows would have risen if they hadn't been prevented by Botox. 'How old fashioned of you, daahling. I shall be an expert who has retired *very* early from a prestigious university and I shall partner the detective in his search for the truth. Maybe there will be a frisson between the expert and the detective.'

'Isn't the detective in his thirties?' said Fi.

Tallulah pursed her lips and tossed her head.

Demi cleared her throat. 'I haven't forgotten your son, Fi. He can be Miss Levantine's grandson.'

'Son,' said Tallulah, lifting her chin and fixing Fi with a hard stare. 'A *little* late in life, perhaps, but nonetheless. Anyhow, I can make this place work.'

She wandered to the film and TV section and picked through the books. 'How lovely: you have some about me here, too. Are these all you have?' She opened a book, traced her finger over a photograph of her younger self relaxing with the crew on a film set, and shivered.

If her face was a large part of her fortune, thought Fi, *it must be hard to know how much it's changed.* 'I'm afraid so,' she said. 'I'm hoping for more to arrive before the play closes.' She waited for a sharp retort, but Tallulah turned her glorious smile on Fi.

'These are *all* one wants.' She snorted daintily. 'And more than Andy Hale or Elsa O'Brien will ever achieve. *They'll* never be in a book, third-rate actors that they are. Amateur Andy and Expressionless Elsa, I call them. They think I don't know they're mocking me, whispering in corners and sniggering like teenagers. Well, when it comes to those two, I'm happy to call a spade a spade. They're careless, shoddy and unskilled, and they don't treat the theatre with respect. It harms all of us.' She moved to the folklore section and picked up a book on sailors' superstitions. 'I'm sure you worry about the same things as we actors do,' she said, pointing at the cover.

'Er…' Fi considered telling Tallulah that she knew more about theatre superstitions than boat ones. But Tallulah had already put the book down and moved on.

'Let's chat, Fi.' Demi patted the sofa. 'No pressure, of course, but let me show you what our scene guy envisages, and the timetable. Perhaps it'll help you see how it will work.' She held out the tablet.

'OK, but only till my son comes home. No final decisions, and if a customer comes in, they take precedence.' With a sigh, Fi sat beside Demi and took the tablet.

Demi leaned in and scrolled through the document, describing which parts would be filmed on the boat, how long the process would take, and how Dylan and maybe Nerys would fit in. Against her better instincts, Fi found herself mesmerised by the images of a Book Barge Plus and dazzled by the excitement of being part of a TV production, with the possibilities it might lead to for Dylan.

There was a sudden yap and Fi looked round. She'd left the door to the living quarters open. She stood up. 'I need to check on my dog.'

She'd said it without thinking. *My dog*. It was no distance, but she hurried.

Tallulah was in the galley and the dog was standing on one of the chairs, yapping at her.

'Hello, daahling,' said Tallulah. 'I just thought I'd see where my character lives.'

'She lives on a different boat where people respect privacy,' retorted Fi. 'I haven't decided about the shop part yet, but nothing whatsoever is being filmed in here.'

'So sorry, daahling,' said Tallulah. 'Come along, Demi.'

She swept out of the living quarters and headed for the steps. With a sigh and an eye-roll, Demi said goodbye to Fi and followed Tallulah.

'*Grr!*' The dog had something in his mouth and was growling through it. Was it an envelope? 'Don't you start messing with my records, too,' said Fi.

He trotted over and offered it to her. 'I should think so,' said Fi, taking it. The envelope had one word typed on it: *Tallulah*. Fi wrinkled her nose as a familiar scent wafted up: a smell that made her faintly nauseous and giddy.

'Tallulah!' she called. 'You've left something behind.'

'Really?' Tallulah paused on the steps. When she saw what Fi was holding she scowled, as far as her face would allow it. 'It must have dropped out of my bag.' She descended and took the letter. 'It's from Andy. Quite the diatribe.' She sniffed, then with a regal wave at Demi she left the boat.

Fi followed, to make sure they actually went ashore and didn't begin poking about on deck. As Tallulah crossed the steady gangplank she stumbled and dropped the letter. It floated, taking on water, and slowly sank. 'Whoops,' said Tallulah.

'Do you want me to try and fish it out?' asked Fi.

'Oh no. I know what it says and I have no desire to read it again. It's failed in its intended purpose.' She beamed at Fi. 'Toodle-oo.'

'That wasn't weird at all, was it?' said Fi to the dog as she peered into the narrow gap between boat and bank. It would be impossible to retrieve the letter without moving *Coralie*. She frowned, her mind whirring.

The dog whined, pawed at his snout as if trying to wipe something away, then bounded onto the bank and retched in the grass.

The scent, thought Fi, as she went to comfort him. *It was the same as the wine. Something really doesn't add up this time. Even I can see that. I just can't work out why.*

CHAPTER 22

Crystal Dreams was, for once, quiet. The after-school rush had died down, and Jade was taking the opportunity to put out some of the stock which had arrived an hour earlier.

Every so often, she giggled. Then she felt bad and said to herself sternly, *It's not her fault.* But at least the mystery was explained.

Geraldine's visit the other day, though intended to persuade Jade to recruit her, had had precisely the opposite effect. The more she boasted of her expertise in pricing and selling, the more Jade remembered the mess she had made of Fi's records – in particular, her misrecording of a certain significant book not so long ago. And the more Geraldine talked of her vital role at the Book Barge, the more Jade thought of her role in disposing of the only real evidence they had: the bottle of poisoned wine.

'I'll think it over,' she had said to Geraldine, with no intention of doing so. In fact she had resolved, if possible, to make Netta a properly official employee. *If I don't, Geraldine may be so busy trying to win me round that she messes Fi's business up even more.*

So when she had come in from a lunchtime walk with Fi, during which they had agreed that they were at a complete standstill on the case, Jade's first impulse was to be sure of *something*. 'Netta, have you thought any more about going on the payroll?'

Netta looked as if Jade was about to rip a plaster off her. After much fiddling with the objects on the counter, she said, 'Yes, I will. But you have to promise not to laugh.'

'Why would I laugh?'

'You'll find out,' said Netta, darkly.

Jade's eyebrows almost climbed into her hairline, but she made tea for them both and fetched her notebook. 'I just need a few details. Full name, national insurance number, that sort of thing.' She had made a list earlier. 'OK, your full name first.'

Netta said nothing. Jade waited, pen poised.

Netta mumbled a response to the counter.

'I'm sorry, I missed that.'

Netta huffed. 'Viennetta Louise Brown.'

Jade managed, with difficulty, to keep a straight face. 'That's unusual,' she said eventually. 'How do you spell it?'

'You know. Like the pudding.' Netta's eyes flashed.

'OK.' Jade wrote it down. 'Can you give me your NI number?'

Netta got up and pulled a crumpled letter out of her bag. 'It's on there.' Jade copied it into her book. 'Don't tell anyone. I mean, everyone I went to school with knows anyway, but no one else. Not even Fi.'

'I won't,' said Jade, and they continued the process. 'I'll check if you need to fill out any forms too, Netta.'

'I didn't realise until I was four,' said Netta. 'An advert came on the TV. At first it was cool, but later, not so much.'

'Your secret is safe with me,' said Jade. At that moment a customer had come in, and they had returned to work.

Jade hung up more charms – surely every resident of Hazeby-on-Wyvern must have one by now – and allowed herself a proper laugh.

'What's so funny?' barked a voice behind her.

Standing inside the doorway was a woman, perhaps in her seventies, wearing a buttoned-up red coat, brogues and walking socks.

'I'm sorry,' Jade said. 'I was just remembering something on the radio earlier.'

'Oh,' said the woman. 'Well, I've come to you as a last resort. I don't hold with any of this witchy-woo stuff, but I believe you're a friend of Fi Booker's and she's normal. Now, I've traipsed to the health-food shop and the price of their herbs has gone up shocking. I don't drive, which means the garden centre's out, so I'm wondering if you can help an old lady.' Her eyes gleamed.

'I might be able to,' said Jade. 'What is it you're after?'

The woman drew a piece of paper from her pocket and unfolded it. 'Evening primrose, echinacea, camomile, St John's wort.'

'Right,' said Jade. 'I don't stock any of those.'

'Call yourself a witch,' said the woman.

'I don't, actually,' said Jade. 'I just happen to run a crystal and magic shop. It's a business. If you need regular supplies of these herbs, I daresay we can do a deal. How much do you want?'

'Now that's what I like to hear.' She went over her requirements, together with a few other herbs she would be interested in acquiring, and Jade wrote them on a fresh page of her notebook.

'Can I take your name and number, please?'

'You may.' The woman took her pen and wrote *Mrs J. Brummell*, pressing heavily on the page, then pulled an antique mobile from her pocket, peered at a label stuck on the back, and added her number. 'Please don't text. Stupid small type.' She slid the notebook and pen back across the counter. 'I'll wait to hear from you.' She looked past Jade and snorted. 'I swear that woman gets where dirt can't.'

Jade turned and saw the photograph of Tallulah and Netta. 'Have you seen the play?'

'No, I have not.' Mrs Brummell made a noise very like a harrumph. 'I had quite enough of Tallulah Levantine at school, thank you. Not that she was in my year. She was a few years above me, not that you'd think it to look at her.' She pushed back the skin on her cheeks until she appeared to be in a wind tunnel.

'Oh really?' said Jade, trying to keep her expression neutral.

'Oh yes,' said Mrs Brummell, and chuckled. 'Not that she was called Tallulah back then. Joan Jones, she was. Granted, she was pretty, but didn't she know it. We were at the girls' grammar, which was next door to the boys' grammar, so you can guess what she spent her time doing. Oh, she was a byword all right.'

Jade considered switching her shop sign to *Closed*, and crossed her fingers that no other customers would disturb them. 'What sort of thing did Tallulah get up to?'

'I've already mentioned the boys. Her blouse was never done up properly, not to mention being at least one size too small. As for her skirts – well! "One day I'll be a star," she used to say. "I won't just be plain Joan Jones." And what's wrong with the name Joan? It's a perfectly good name.'

Jade looked at the notebook where Mrs Brummell

had written her details. 'It is. A much nicer name than Tallulah.'

'She wanted the lead in every school play,' said Mrs Brummell. 'The drama mistress couldn't stand her, though. Our school put on *Romeo and Juliet* with the boys' school, which is a risky decision if you ask me, and of course Tallulah had to be Juliet. But Miss Bainton wasn't having it. She made Tallulah the understudy and gave the role of Juliet to Hattie Marsh. Hattie was a lovely girl and she'd won the prize for spoken verse the previous year, so she was a good choice. Tallulah was told she'd be out of the whole thing if she made any trouble, and she calmed down. Or so we thought.' Her eyes gleamed again. 'Everything went like clockwork till Hattie had a nasty case of upset tummy before the dress rehearsal. She was a game girl and she did her best, but you can't have Juliet vomiting over the front row, can you?'

'No, indeed,' said Jade. *My role is one of willing listener*, she thought. *I'm more than happy to play that part.*

'So of course, Miss Bainton didn't have a choice. Tallulah took the stage and gave it her all. There were rumours that she gave young Romeo her all as well, but I'm not in a position to comment. Oh yes, and somehow the drama critic from a London newspaper was in the audience. He raved about her and a star was born, as they say.'

'Gosh,' said Jade. 'So that was the beginning of Tallulah's career?'

'It was, though we didn't know that,' said Mrs Brummell. 'As soon as Hattie could keep down a piece of dry toast, she was back in and Tallulah was out. But there was no London critic for Hattie. Oh, Tallulah was full of herself. The mistresses tried to cut her down to size, but she wasn't having it. The next thing, it was all round the school that Tallulah had run away from home, two months before she was due to do her O-levels. Naturally, the headmistress, without naming names, held her up as a bad example. A girl who was sure to come to grief through her vanity and impulsive actions, she said, and would never be heard of again.' She laughed. 'Less than a year later, everyone had heard of Tallulah. She was on the posters at the local cinema – mind you, in those days I was too young to watch the film she was in – and if anything, her blouse had got smaller and her skirt even shorter. So if she has come to grief, *I* haven't seen it.' She unleashed another snort. 'You'd never have thought it, but Tallulah was smarter than anyone gave her credit for.'

Another customer came in and wandered towards the cauldrons. 'What makes you say that, Mrs Brummell?' asked Jade. 'I mean, surely most of that was luck.'

Mrs Brummell regarded her with narrowed eyes. 'You seem like a smart woman to me,' she said. 'One who understands how things work, and knows what side her bread's buttered on. Bit like Tallulah, if you don't mind me saying.'

'She's certainly a strong woman,' said Jade. 'And a survivor. But I still think that some of what you've told me was down to luck.' She willed Mrs Brummell to take the bait.

'Maybe you're right,' said Mrs Brummell. 'Maybe it's coincidence that when I went to the post office for a pennorth of sweets, two days before the first night of *Romeo and Juliet*, Tallulah was in there sending a telegram. And perhaps it means nothing that on the day Hattie had an upset tummy, Tallulah had offered her the last sherbet lemon in her bag of sweets.' She fixed Jade with a triumphant look. 'I'll leave you to draw your own conclusions. Don't forget to ring me about those herbs.'

'No, I won't.' Jade tapped her notebook. 'Thank you very much, Mrs Brummell.'

'What for?' Mrs Brummell smiled a slow smile. 'I haven't said I'll buy anything from you yet. It depends whether your price is good.'

Jade smiled back at her. 'I'm thanking you for giving me the chance,' she said. 'I'll be in touch as soon as I can.'

'I'm sure you will,' said Mrs Brummell, and

stomped out of the shop.

Jade salved her businesswoman's conscience by calling 'Let me know if you need any help!' to her browsing customer, then pulled the notebook towards her and began to scribble. *It's becoming clearer,* she thought as she wrote, careless of anything except getting down what Mrs Brummell had said. *But the question is, why?*

CHAPTER 23

'What wine would you recommend with this?' said Jade. She scrutinised her burger doubtfully and took a hesitant nibble.

'Vin de plutonium,' said Fi. 'I swear these chik'not veggie nuggets are radioactive.'

The glare of an overhead strip light bouncing off Cheeky Chik'n's red and yellow walls cast a weird glow on the food. It was hard to know how even a teenager could want to eat there, but it was the last place anyone would expect to see Jade and Fi, so they could talk without being overheard. The teenagers were staring into phone screens while K-pop blasted from the TV over the counter.

Jade extracted a piece of lettuce from her burger and contemplated it. 'The last time I saw anything this shade of green, it was my hair during a punk phase. Never mind anyone else trying to poison us, we can do it all by ourselves.'

'I don't think anyone was trying to poison anyone,' said Fi. 'Not to death, anyway. I think it was something to make the recipient feel ill and under threat. The envelope was probably sprayed with whatever it was to remind the recipient of the smell.' She put her half-eaten nugget down and pushed a plastic wallet across the table. 'This isn't my idea of a diatribe.' Inside the wallet was a damp, smeared envelope and a cleaner, marginally drier card of the type that florists put with bouquets. In neat biro it said: *It should have been you. A x*

'The police will never get anything useful off those,' said Jade. 'They're less use than this bottle.' She patted the battered boot standing on the chair next to her. 'I'd have paid good money to watch you teetering on the edge of *Coralie,* fishing with the boat hook.'

'I was attached to the rail,' said Fi. 'I'm not a fool. I couldn't have fallen in. And I'd never have got it if it hadn't snagged in a bit of driftwood. The point isn't just getting it analysed for poison, it's the envelope and the note itself. Tallulah's name is typed with a typewriter – wonky letters and everything. Who types nowadays? Who owns a typewriter? And Tallulah hinted that the note was a threat from Andy. But why type the envelope and write the card? And who would put a kiss on a threatening note?'

'A sarcastic psychopath with a nasty sense of humour?' said Jade, taking a swig of diet cola. 'I can't see it, not from Andy. What seems more likely is that Andy gave a bunch of flowers to Elsa, to cheer her up after missing out on Lady Macbeth. The card that came with the bouquet has been reused to sound like a threat. The kiss at the end gives it away.' She tapped her notebook. 'If someone has enough drive, they can do pretty much anything. For example, grammar-school girl to film star in a few short, mini-skirted steps. Have you seen any of Tallulah's films yet? I've just seen a few stills from the cheesy horrors, where she keeps forgetting how much clothing to wear.'

'I found a pirated version of her last classic online and downloaded it for us to look at,' said Fi, tapping on her tablet and handing it over. 'I had a quick scan but I couldn't see anything useful. Maybe you can. I want to check through Tallulah's autobiography. It finally arrived this afternoon.'

'Did that fall in the river too?' said Jade, eyeing the battered hardback that Fi put on the table. The dust jacket had rips and tears, but the front cover was fairly pristine: a monochrome photograph of a young Tallulah, head tilted, eyes wide, lips parted, under the title *TALLULAH – A LIFE*.

Fi turned the pages. 'I've never liked celebrity autobiographies. They're usually only unique till the person hits puberty and then it's predictable. When they get famous, it's all name-dropping. And to write one when you're' – she checked the back cover – 'twenty-two seems so pretentious. I suppose she'd lived a bit more than the average person, but... This must have come out just before she changed direction in her career, then disappeared into obscurity.' Fi flicked through the pages and paused at the photographs. Tallulah on stage undertaking classical roles; Tallulah on film and TV sets, in period costume; Tallulah on the sets of her two classic films in psychedelic dresses and long boots, smoking; Tallulah relaxing with friends, dolled up to the nines. 'There's nothing in here to suggest she's anything other than a serious actress with a great future. Nothing obvious to suggest she was thinking of moving into less arty films. What changed?'

'Were those "less arty" films banned when they came out?' said Jade, squinting at the tablet. 'Or censored, at least?'

'Not by 1970,' said Fi. 'But the public can be hypocritical. They might enjoy the films, but if she became a byword for tackiness no one would take her or this book seriously. It was probably remaindered pretty quickly. It was almost impossible to get a copy.'

'What does she say about school?'

'Mmm... Just a chapter which mentions her being spotted as Juliet,' said Fi. 'Nothing to suggest that she got the role by anything other than raw talent.' She turned back to the photographs. In the social shots, several young men were hanging around her. With their long, sleek hair and heavy moustaches and beards, none looked familiar. 'What's baffling me is that Tallulah wrote this book and never asked me why I didn't stock it. Yet it's all about her, rather than featuring a number of actresses of whom she's one. But she hinted strongly that she didn't want me to stock anything other than what I had.'

Fi started to read again, then her phone burst into life. Andy was video-calling her. She stared at the phone for a second, showed it to Jade, then answered, moving so that it would be hard for him to work out where she was. 'Hello?'

'Hi,' said Andy. 'Er . . . where are you?'

'Grabbing a snack before coming to the theatre. What's up?'

'I wanted to apologise for being weird,' he said. 'And to explain something in case you hear it another way, things being what they are. I sent Elsa some flowers with a note to say I was sorry she wasn't in the right role, and I put a kiss at the end of the note by accident. I thought it was best to be upfront about it. I swear Elsa's just a friend.'

'I believe you,' said Fi. 'Was the card in a large typed envelope?'

'A what?' said Andy. 'Florists don't use large envelopes or typewriters. In fact, the only typewriter

I've seen for years is a prop at the theatre. It's a beast.' He laughed. 'Charles wants me to use it in our next play, so I tried it out the other day. I was rubbish. I'll have to thump random keys and hope it's convincing. Why do you ask?'

'No reason,' said Fi. 'Andy, when Charles hit you – had you arranged to meet him?'

Andy pulled a face. 'Not exactly,' he said. 'I'd been texting him. Looking back, I was a bit full of myself. I got carried away with what I thought might happen for me and for Elsa, and it got his goat. They had a row, but I didn't know that till afterwards. Anyway, he texted and said he'd like to meet me to talk over the performance, and that was when he accused me of trying it on with Elsa and walloped me. Then a couple of days later, he asked if I was the "fan" who'd left a bottle of Greek wine for Elsa. I said no. I'd seen a bottle of Greek wine, but that was in Tallulah's locker: I saw her putting it behind her stuff. None of my business: she's never shown any signs of being drunk on stage, or even merry. Anyway, at least Charles believed me about that. He said, "Good, I'll give it to her, then". If he doesn't know Elsa's not keen on red wine by now, that's not my problem. She probably cooked with it.'

Jade leaned into the shot, brandishing the bottle of wine. 'Was this the one you saw Tallulah stashing?'

'Er, hi, Jade. Yes, I think so. Why do you have it?'

Andy frowned, then shook his head. 'Look, never mind. Fi, can we talk later? I'm worried, really worried. I just want to know someone's on my side. That Inspector Falconer...' He checked his watch. 'I have to go. But can we meet?'

'I'll see what I can do,' said Fi. 'Bye.' She closed the call.

Jade was scribbling more notes. 'The inspector will arrive in a few minutes,' she said. 'Do we tell him all this, too? Did Tallulah leave the bottle anonymously for Charles to give to Elsa? If so, why? Genuine admiration, or guilt because she'd taken the part of Lady Macbeth?'

'She doesn't seem the type,' said Fi.

'Did someone prompt Tallulah to give it to us? At what point did it get contaminated, and who was the intended victim? Unless someone confesses, how will we know?'

'We're missing something.' Fi picked up the book again and peered at a photograph of Tallulah. This time, she was draped over a young man. Even with his hippyish beard it was possible to tell that he was younger than she was, perhaps in his late teens. The background didn't seem British. The sky was a bright Mediterranean blue, and in the background was a swimming pool backed by olive trees. The caption read: *True love at last with Ioannis, my fiancé and guiding angel.* 'Look.' She turned the book so that

Jade could see it.

'Interesting,' said Jade. 'Just a second...' She paused the film she'd been watching and scrolled to the end. 'I saw something when I was whizzing through... In the credits, there's a thank-you to a Georgios Angelis. A backer? And here's Ioannis Angelis: junior production assistant.'

Fi picked up her napkin and covered the man's beard with it. 'That's Jon Angel, I swear it.'

'You're right,' said Jade. 'The photo of Jon Angel's son in the paper looked just like that. So . . . Jon and Tallulah were once engaged. Is that why he was in her dressing room? Old times' sake?'

'Or something else?' said Fi.

'I did suggest a pub next time,' said Inspector Falconer, sitting down next to Fi with a bump and eyeing her veggie nuggets with barely concealed disgust. 'Apart from anything else, the food and the music's better.'

'You're still making me jump.'

'You're still making me doubt my sanity. I've got a case to solve at the theatre, you know. Someone's been cross-checking mobile messages and we've found some, shall we say, unexpected fingerprints on Jon Angel's phone. I have to get down there. Please don't tell me you think Cheeky Chk'n is implicated in this, too.'

'Nope,' said Jade, handing him the boot.

'What the—?'

'It's something to analyse. We should have given it to you a couple of days ago, but we weren't sure it was relevant. Now we are. Not the boot: what's inside. And these.' She pushed over the plastic wallet. 'They're all relevant. Possibly poisoned, or made to look as if they were. And the typewriter at the theatre needs dusting, too.' The inspector opened his mouth. 'Before you say anything, this is not us adding things up wrong. This time, we're adding them up right.'

'Us? We?' He sighed. 'Not again.'

'Yes,' said Jade. 'I suppose we ought to explain.'

Inspector Falconer rolled his eyes. 'That would be nice,' he said. 'And once you have, I hope you'll let me get on with my investigation. I'm very close.'

'But you're close to the wrong person,' said Fi. 'You might as well get yourself something to drink, Inspector. This will take a while.'

CHAPTER 24

'Are you sure this will work?' asked Fi.

'I don't see any reason why not,' Jade replied. 'Hold still, will you? You're making this even more difficult.'

'Look at it this way,' said Inspector Falconer, who was observing the scene with interest. 'If it doesn't work, it doesn't matter. You can sneak off, and as far as anybody will know, it was just a silly prank.'

'Maybe,' said Fi.

'The thing is, this is our best chance,' said Jade. 'It's the last rehearsal, for the performance they're going to film.'

'Jade's right,' said the inspector, and they both looked at him in surprise. 'I'm sorry to put you under pressure, Fi, but we don't have enough solid evidence. There's too much hearsay, and this has to be watertight.'

'Why does it have to be me?' Fi turned to Jade. 'You could do it. You'd probably enjoy it.'

'I'm the stage manager. Besides, you're all ready.'

Inspector Falconer put a hand on Fi's arm. 'If you really don't want to, Fi, you don't have to,' he said. 'But it could be a great help. If it works, Andy Hale is off the hook.'

'I suppose,' said Fi, with a slight scowl.

'I can hear people leaving the dressing rooms,' said Jade. 'We'd better get going. Inspector, you know what you have to do?'

'I've committed my role to memory,' said the inspector. 'Take my position and wait for a text message. And yes, everyone's been warned.'

'Wonderful. Fi, got what you need?'

Fi nodded.

'Just a moment.' Jade checked the curtains were closed, then switched off the light. 'Do your thing, Fi.'

A strange noise came from Inspector Falconer.

'Lovely,' said Jade, with satisfaction.

***

Charles got up from his seat in the front row and clapped his hands. 'Right, everybody, let's get on with it. I daresay you'd rather be somewhere else, but this is important. Tonight the production will be filmed, and I want you all to appear to your best advantage. I'm sure you want that, too.'

The cast made noises of general agreement. They

were dressed in casual, comfortable clothing apart from Tallulah, who was in full costume.

'OK, there are a few key points to look at, then we'll go for a complete run-through. Act one, scene five. Tallulah, take it from the top.'

Tallulah stepped forward and wrinkled her nose. 'What's that smell?'

'I don't smell anything,' said Charles, and Jade smiled as she peeked from her hiding place in one of the balcony boxes. Her investment in a bottle of 'Zombie for Her' perfume, and spritzing the front of the stage with it, had paid off.

Tallulah stood centre stage, the tartan shawl thrown casually over one shoulder. 'Do I need my letter prop?'

'Just pretend you're holding a letter,' said Charles, wearily. 'OK, take it away.'

Jade made sure her phone was on silent and typed a text: *Any time in the next 2 minutes.* She pressed send and watched the stage. Tallulah got through her opening speech, then dismissed the messenger and advanced.

'The raven himself is hoarse
That croaks the fatal entrance of Duncan—'

The auditorium was plunged into darkness.

Tallulah shrieked, and there were a few cries from the wings.

'Don't worry,' called Charles. 'It's probably a

loose connection. Can someone sort it, please? And if the spotlights are working, can we get one on Tallulah?'

'I'll go and take a look,' said a gruff voice.

'Thanks, Terry. If you wouldn't mind carrying on, Tallulah. We've a lot to get through.'

Tallulah said nothing until a single spotlight illuminated her. She started her speech again, but this time her voice was less confident, her posture stiff. *'Come, thick night—'* She gasped, her eyes wide and terrified, her jaw slack. 'What – what is it?'

'What's *what*, Tallulah?' asked Charles.

'That – that *thing!*' Tallulah pointed a trembling finger into the darkness of the auditorium. 'It's coming towards me! Ohhh!'

'I don't see anything,' said Charles. 'Can anyone else see something in the auditorium?'

'Not me,' said Andy's voice, from the wings.

'It's gone now,' said Tallulah, but she still seemed haunted.

'Jolly good,' said Charles. 'Now, if you wouldn't mind—'

'This is what comes of disregarding the old traditions,' said Tallulah, with resentment in her voice. 'Look what happened when someone switched off the ghost light – I could have died if that light had hit me! And as for whatever idiot broke a mirror earlier…'

'You can pick up from where you left off,' said Charles.

Tallulah heaved a sigh and struck an attitude.

'Come, thick night,
And pall thee in the dunnest smoke of hell,
That my keen knife see not the wound it makes—'

She screamed and fell to her knees. And well she might, for on stage, perhaps ten feet away from her, floated a death's head.

'You know all about knives, don't you, Tallulah?' The voice was unearthly, inhuman.

Tallulah scrambled backwards and the spotlight followed her. 'Someone save me! You don't know what happened!'

The skull said nothing, then glided towards Tallulah. *'Tell me,'* it said, and Tallulah quaked.

'He cheated me,' she said. 'He *ruined* me.'

'Who?'

'Everyone thinks Jon Angel was a pillar of the establishment, but when I first met him, he was nothing. A glorified runner. Once he was with me, I introduced him to people and lent him money – a lot of money – to realise his dreams. I even backed some of his early productions, more fool me. And once Jon's position was secure, how did he repay me? He left me. Worse – he made a joke of me, till no reputable casting director would give me a second look. Do you know how it feels to beg for a margarine commercial? For a walk-on part as the elderly housekeeper?'

She rose, stepped forward and faced the auditorium as if delivering her greatest lines. 'Jon Angel ruined me, and I swore that one day I would make him pay. Oh, it was easy in the end. An invitation to my dressing room after the show for a private chat about a promising young director I'd met, a glass of something to relax him, then—' She gripped an imaginary dagger and drove it home. 'I got my revenge at last for all those years I spent in the wilderness, and I'm not sorry. The sight of his face as the dagger went in was worth it.'

She smiled at the memory. 'As for the rest of you —' She gazed into the darkness. 'How easy you were to fool. A hint here, a titbit there, and you were at each other's throats. Oh, the vanity.' Her lip curled. 'Jon actually unlocked his phone for me to put my number in it. Little did he know that I was sending a text to Andy – the text that would put him under suspicion and me in the clear.'

Someone coughed. Tallulah scowled, as if annoyed at being interrupted, spread her arms wide and thrust her chest towards the apparition. 'Take me now!'

The skull moved backwards, then disappeared. Tallulah let out a whimper, her face full of fear.

A sound came from the wings and grew louder. The sound of a person applauding.

With measured footsteps, Inspector Falconer strode into the spotlight. 'Tallulah, thank you for giving me my cue. Tallulah Levantine, alias Joan Jones, I am arresting you for the murder of Jon Angel.' He paused and looked around him, into the darkness. 'I'll do the rest of it in a minute, but could somebody please put the lights back on?'

'On it, guvnor,' said a voice that Jade recognised from the Swan. Thirty seconds later, everyone blinked as the lights flickered on. Most of the cast had left the wings and were staring at Tallulah. Standing to one side, wearing a black cloak which didn't go with her jeans and jumper, was Fi.

'What's *she* doing here?' Tallulah said, accusingly. 'This is meant to be a closed rehearsal.'

Fi grinned, then held a small torch under her chin and switched it on. Instantly, a glowing skull was superimposed on her features. 'You can call me . . . *the fourth witch.*'

Jade stood up and leaned over the edge of her box. 'Ultraviolet make-up, Tallulah,' she called. 'It's invisible except in black light. Oh, and a voice changer.'

Tallulah stared at her, then turned back to Fi. 'You were in league with *him!*' she cried, stabbing a finger at Andy.

Inspector Falconer stepped forward. 'Miss Levantine, I haven't finished your caution, but you don't have to say anything, especially if it will further incriminate you.'

'I don't care!' Tallulah shouted. 'Andy never wanted me in this production; he made that perfectly clear, and so did Elsa. They couldn't bear the limelight being taken from them. So when I was looking for someone to take the blame, the choice was clear. You laughed at me behind my back, and you weren't much more polite to my face.' She stalked towards Andy, her fist raised, and he backed away. 'How dare you,' she said, through clenched teeth. 'You small-time actor, you middle manager, you *hobbyist*!' She rounded on Elsa. 'And you're no better! The only reason you even got Lady Macduff was because of Charles. Anywhere else, you'd be understudying and thankful for it!'

Andy and Elsa exchanged glances and shrugged. 'At least we're not murderers,' said Andy.

Tallulah glared at him, her chest heaving.

'Right,' said Charles, from the front row, and everybody turned towards him. 'This has been most entertaining, and I'm glad the matter has been brought to a satisfactory conclusion, but unless you've all forgotten, the show must go on. Inspector, would you do the necessary?'

'It'll be a pleasure,' said Inspector Falconer, and drew a set of handcuffs from his pocket. 'Don't make me use these, Miss Levantine. And don't try to run for it: officers are stationed at every exit.'

Tallulah didn't move. 'So that's it?' she said to Charles, her eyes wide with disbelief. 'You're going to let this man take me away and put your precious play in the hands of *these* two?' She dismissed Andy and Elsa with a wave of her hand.

Charles grinned. 'You betcha. Elsa, are you ready?'

Elsa stepped forward. 'Born ready,' she said, and beamed.

'Good,' said Charles. 'Let's take it from the top and see how we get on. Might be a long afternoon, but we'll get there.'

'But – but—' Tallulah looked pleadingly at the stage as Inspector Falconer led her off.

Jade hastened to the foyer, arriving just before the inspector. Constable Jeavons was waiting by the theatre doors. She brightened when she saw Jade. 'Oh, hello.'

'Excellent work, Ms Fitch,' said the inspector, smiling at her.

Jade smiled back. 'You can call me Jade, you know.'

'Indeed. Most ingenious, Jade. I'm glad you're on our side. Constable Jeavons, get them to bring the car round, would you?' He turned to Tallulah. 'Or would you prefer to leave via the stage door?'

Tallulah flung up her head. 'Certainly not. What sort of exit is *that*?' And she practically dragged the inspector past Constable Jeavons. As she flung open the door, Inspector Falconer looked over his shoulder and winked at Jade.

'He's in a good mood,' said Constable Jeavons.

It took Jade a moment to recover from the wink. 'He should be,' she said, eventually. 'A murder, an attack and an attempted poisoning all cleared up in one fell swoop.'

Fi came into the foyer. 'They've gone, then,' she said.

'You just missed him,' said Jade. 'But I'm sure your paths will cross again.'

Fi ran a finger down her cheek and examined it critically. 'I should have asked you this beforehand, but is this stuff easy to remove? I don't want to glow in the dark for the next week.'

'Don't worry.' Jade reached into her pocket and put a small bottle in Fi's hand. 'The instructions are on there. And anyway…'

'What?' said Fi, frowning.

Jade grinned. 'You could always leave the light on.'

CHAPTER 25

The river ran past *Coralie*, reflections of the night sky and coloured lights rippling, merging and separating as it flowed. Jade's neighbour Rick's folk trio was playing 'Hunter Moon' on the foredeck, and the haunting words flowed through Fi's mind as she stared into the water, where the real moon fractured into silver slivers on the waves.

'Earth calling Fi,' said Andy. He held out a glass of mulled wine, the steam coiling into the air. 'You look as if you're about to transform into an otter and swim away.'

'Too cold, and I don't like raw fish,' said Fi. She took the wine and sipped it, watching the people on the boat. Some were chattering, some swaying to the folk music, all coloured with harlequin lights. The party was pretty nearly perfect.

Jade was sitting with Dylan and his friends,

apparently engaged in whatever Chloe was saying, but Fi could tell she was trying not to laugh. Nerys was rocking her sleepy son to the music. Elsa and Charles were slow dancing, arms wrapped around each other, spinning in their own world. Every now and then, Elsa's engagement ring sparkled in a beam of light.

Stuart and his husband Xander were chatting with Inspector Falconer – Marcus – and Marcus was laughing. Fi wondered what the joke was. Perhaps aware that he was being observed, he looked over at her and Andy and his laugh faded into a smile. He raised his bottle of beer and Fi raised her mulled wine in response.

Netta and Mrs Brummell were sitting with...

Fi realised that Andy was still speaking and refocused. 'Sorry, what?'

'I *said*, I heard back from that TV company.'

'Angel Productions?'

'Yes, of course.' He sounded peevish. 'I thought you'd be interested.'

'I am,' said Fi. 'What did they say?' In her mind, she crossed her fingers. Andy deserved a break. The last twelve years had been hard for him, the last few weeks a nightmare. He was a good actor. He just needed someone to give him a chance.

'They're making a new private-detective series set in London,' he said. 'A bit darker than *Meadows of Murder*. It's already in the works, but someone dropped out. They've asked me to be in the detective's team. Not her sidekick, but in every episode, in lots of scenes. It might not take off, but then again it might. And if it does, I could get promoted in the second series. I could even become the sidekick.'

'Wow!' said Fi. 'That's wonderful! What happens next?'

'They want me in London on Monday.'

'Congratulations! I'm really pleased for you!' Fi gave him a one-armed hug. Andy hugged her back, tighter, and kissed the top of her head. She wriggled. 'Watch out for my wine. The stains would be a nightmare to get out of the deck.'

Andy let her go, looking at her quizzically. 'I've put my place on the market and I'll see what I can buy in London. A shoebox, probably. It's a risk, but it feels like now or never. Do you understand?'

'Of course,' said Fi. 'That's how I felt when I decided to buy *Coralie* and move here.'

'There's a river in London,' said Andy, his head on one side. 'A book barge could do very well.'

Fi took a gulp of wine and scanned the boat. She caught Jade's eye, raised her eyebrows as high as they would go, then turned back to Andy, her expression normal. 'There's already a book barge near Kings Cross,' she said. 'Maybe others, too.'

'Yeah, but... Things between us were just getting going. They took a bit of a diversion, but— Oh, hi

Jade.' He sighed.

'Heaven preserve me from teenagers,' said Jade, clinking her glass of warm, spiced rum with Fi and Andy's glasses of mulled wine. 'If that Chloe doesn't start angling for a job as soon as she's sixteen, I'm a mermaid.'

'Would that be a bad thing?' asked Fi.

'It will be if she's still pumping me for my trade secrets.'

'Trade secrets?'

'My skills in the magic arts.'

'You haven't got any.'

Andy chuckled. '*Everyone* knows that Jade conjured up the Head of the Goddess of Justice in the theatre with her hocus-pocus.'

'Pfft,' said Jade. 'Anyone with an ounce of common sense knows that's hogwash. Sadly, that doesn't include fifty per cent of the townsfolk and ninety-nine per cent of the teenagers. Even the people who were actually in the theatre doubt what they saw. It's ridiculous.' She grinned. 'But super good for business. Cheers!' She clinked glasses with Fi again. 'All we need is for Fi to find a replacement for Geraldine, now she's gone to work at that herbal place, where she'll tell *them* how to do everything.'

'I'll be OK, actually,' said Fi, 'because—'

'Excellent,' said Andy. 'Can we—'

'Oh yes!' said Fi. 'Guess what? Andy's got a TV

role. He's moving to London.'

'Wow! Celebrations all round, then!'

'Fi and I were just—'

'Hunter Moon' came to an end and everyone clapped. From the other boats and the people walking on the towpath came applause, cheers and cries of 'More!'

'Thank you, thank you!' called Rick through the microphone. 'Now for one last slow song before we finish the night with a bang. Something a bit mysterious this time: "She Walked Through The Fair".'

'Rick's great,' said Fi. 'I'm so glad you found out he had a band, Jade.'

'Once he'd finished talking about marquetry, he told me all about it,' said Jade. 'He'd soundproofed the office in his shop so that he could practise without me hearing.'

'That's odd,' said Fi. 'He didn't mind you hearing him saw wood, or whatever he does.'

'That's different, I guess.' said Jade. 'Work, not personal.' She grimaced. 'He says it drowns out what he calls my tortured-whale music.'

'Maybe the two of you could work out how to soundproof between the shops?' said Fi.

'Oh, I dunno. I've got used to the sawing. It's sort of company.' A contemplative smile settled on Jade's face. 'Anyway. I'm glad his band's good. When does the witching hour kick in?'

'If by that you mean how late did the council say I could have music playing outdoors, eleven o'clock. Half an hour left.'

'Shame.'

'Er, Fi?' said Andy, jerking his head towards the tiny area where Elsa and Charles were dancing. 'Could we—'

'Rrrerrfff!' The dog wove his way through legs and chairs and put his front paws on Fi's legs, tail wagging. The young man in the hoodie, who'd been sitting with Mrs Brummell and Netta, followed at a slow lope.

Fi bent to ruffle the dog's head. Andy rolled his eyes and addressed the young man. 'Zach, is it? I hear you're the dog's owner. Fi will be sad to see him go, but it's probably for the best.'

'I'm Zach, yeah, but he's my granddad's dog, not mine. Granddad used to tramp. He'd write sometimes to say where he was, and if we could, Mum and I would meet up with him. Every few years he'd return to Hazeby. But this time, he was really ill. Now he's stuck in a home and he's not happy about it.' Zach managed a smile, but it was a sad one. 'We reckon he'll escape one way or another. Probably the other, but he thinks of that as a new world to tramp.'

'Oh, right,' said Andy. 'I'm sorry. Um . . . at least you'll have the dog to remind you. How long were they together?'

'Not that long. A few months ago we had word that he was twenty miles away and his old dog had passed. So we took him this one, and told Granddad about the book barge to get him to visit. He loves books, and he said he'd like to see it. We reckon he knew he was ill when he came back, and wanted to say goodbye to the place he started from. That night, he told the dog to stay on the barge; he said that anyone who loved books would do the right thing. Then he camped under a bridge, thinking he'd go in the night. I dunno why he didn't contact us, but that's Granddad for you.'

'The dog will be happy with you, though,' said Andy.

'Oh, but he's staying here,' Zach knelt to stroke the dog. 'He'll be happier on a boat than in a poky house. It's fate, anyway. Granddad called him Books, but the farm where he came from called him Stanley, like my granddad. Fi says—'

'Rrrerrfff!'

Fi laughed. 'In my head, as soon as I saw his grey fur, I thought of a wolf. Then I thought of St Wulfstan, the little grey church downriver, and it just seemed to fit. He'll probably be Stan for everyday.'

'Yes, but—' said Andy.

'And I can see him whenever I want,' said Zach, 'because Fi's giving me a trial as an assistant. I didn't get many exams at school, but I love reading and I'm a quick learner. No one's given me a chance before – I can't wait. Anyway, let's get some biscuits, Stan, and let these people talk.'

The music drew to its sad end and Rick spoke into the microphone. 'Enough of the slow stuff – let's raise the skies for the last quarter of an hour! Get on your feet! Young or old, it doesn't matter what your feet are doing. You can all dance to this!' The fiddler burst into a rapid jig and Rick strummed an accompaniment. After a moment's hesitation, everyone got up and began to move towards the gangplank, giggling as they headed for the river bank where there was more space.

Marcus walked over. 'May I have the pleasure, Jade?' he said, crooking his arm. 'I suspect Fi and Andy would like some quiet time.'

'Darn,' said Jade, 'I left my dancing shoes at home. But yeah, go on.'

They made their way onto the grass and started to dance, Jade's Doc Martens kicking and her long skirt floating as she spun. Stan stood and barked, wagging his tail.

Fi led Andy to the side of the boat to watch the dancers revelling under the clear, starry sky. She looked over their heads at Hazeby, glowing with street lights and bright windows.

'You know what I've been trying to say,' said

Andy. 'If you came with me to London, we could see how it goes. You could leave the barge here till you decide.' But good actor as he was, he didn't sound as if he was even convincing himself. He sighed. 'It won't work, will it?'

Fi put her arm round his waist and kissed his cheek. 'No,' she said. 'I'm sorry. We'd make each other miserable. We both have dreams, but they're not the same. You'll make it as an actor this time, I just know it, but not with me. And . . . I can't go back to city life. Hazeby is my home. I'm happy here.'

Andy sighed. His eyes closed briefly, then opened again. He smiled, and to her surprise, the smile was real. 'You're right. I've been fooling myself. Now you've said that, somehow I feel free – how weird is that?' He held her gaze for a long moment. 'Still friends?'

'Still friends,' said Fi.

'Then let's dance. Reckon they'd do a slow one for us to say goodbye?'

'Nah,' said Fi. 'This is a celebration and it's farewell, not goodbye. Everyone's where they should be, or on the way there. Let's go and have some fun.'

WHAT TO READ NEXT

The next book in the Booker & Fitch series is *Murder at Midnight*.

When Jade decides to photograph the winter solstice sunrise at the local stone circle she finds something much less attractive: a dead body.

The body is identified as that of a local businessman. Suspicion immediately falls on the local pagan community, but is everything what it seems?

As the case remains unsolved, Jade's involvement puts her under suspicion and her shop at risk.

Can Jade and Fi uncover the truth – and convince the town they're right?

Check out *Murder at Midnight* at https://mybook.to/MidnightB.

If you've enjoyed reading a co-written book, Caster and Fleet Mysteries is a six-book series we wrote together, set in 1890s London. Meet Katherine and Connie, two young women who become friends in the course of solving a mystery together. Their unlikely partnership takes them to the music hall, masked balls, and beyond. Expect humour, a touch of romance, and above all, shenanigans!

The first book in the series is *The Case of the Black Tulips,* and you can read all about it here: http://mybook.to/Tulips.

If you love modern cozy mysteries set in rural England, *Pippa Parker Mysteries* is another six-book series set in and around the village of Much Gadding.

In the first book, *Murder at the Playgroup*, Pippa is a reluctant newcomer to the village. When she meets the locals, she's absolutely sure. There's just one problem; she's eight months pregnant.

The village is turned upside down when a pillar of the community is found dead at Gadding Goslings playgroup. No one could have murdered her except the people who were there. Everyone's a suspect, including Pippa...

With a baby due any minute, and hampered by her toddler son, can Pippa unmask the murderer?

Find *Murder at the Playgroup* here: http://mybook.to/playgroup.

Finally, if you love books and magic, welcome to

the *Magical Bookshop*! This six-book series combines mystery, magic, cats and of course books, and is set in modern London.

When Jemma James takes a job at Burns Books, the second-worst secondhand bookshop in London, she finds her ambition to turn it around thwarted at every step. Raphael, the owner, is more interested in his newspaper than sales. Folio the bookshop cat has it in for Jemma, and the shop itself appears to have a mind of its own. Or is it more than that?

The first in the series, *Every Trick in the Book*, is here: http://mybook.to/bookshop1

ACKNOWLEDGEMENTS

Our first thanks, as always, go to our superb beta readers – Carol Bissett, Ruth Cunliffe, Christine Downes, Stephen Lenhardt, Carmen Radtke and Julia Smith – and to our keen-eyed and indefatigable proofreader, John Croall. Thank you all for your feedback and suggestions! Any errors that remain are our responsibility.

In case you're wondering, the book barge that Fi mentions at the end of this book is the wonderful Word on the Water book boat in Kings Cross, London. Check it out here: https://wordonthewater.co.uk.

And of course, many thanks to you, our reader! We hope you've enjoyed this book. If you have, please consider leaving a review or rating on Amazon and/or Goodreads. Reviews and ratings are really important to authors, as they help books find new readers.

COVER CREDITS

Image: Depositphotos.

Cover fonts:
Fairing by Design and Co.
Dancing Script OT by Impallari Type: https://www.fontsquirrel.com/fonts/dancing-script-ot. License: SIL Open Font License v1.10: http://scripts.sil.org/OFL.

ABOUT LIZ HEDGECOCK

Liz Hedgecock grew up in London, England, did an English degree, and then took forever to start writing. After several years working in the National Health Service, some short stories crept into the world. A few even won prizes. Then the stories started to grow longer…

Now Liz travels between the nineteenth and twenty-first centuries, murdering people. To be fair, she does usually clean up after herself.

Liz's reimaginings of Sherlock Holmes, her Pippa Parker cozy mystery series, the Caster & Fleet Victorian mystery series (with Paula Harmon), the Magical Bookshop series, and the Maisie Frobisher Mysteries are available in ebook and paperback.

Liz lives in Cheshire with her husband and two sons, and when she's not writing or child-wrangling you can usually find her reading, messing about on

Twitter, or cooing over stuff in museums and art galleries. That's her story, anyway, and she's sticking to it.

Website/blog: http://lizhedgecock.wordpress.com
Facebook: http://www.facebook.com/lizhedgecockwrites
Twitter: http://twitter.com/lizhedgecock
Goodreads: https://www.goodreads.com/lizhedgecock

ABOUT PAULA HARMON

Paula Harmon is a civil servant, living in Dorset, married with two adult children. Paula has several writing projects underway and wonders where the housework fairies are, because the house is a mess and she can't think why.

For book news, offers and even the occasional recipe, please sign up to my newsletter via my website.

https://paulaharmon.com
viewauthor.at/PHAuthorpage
https://www.facebook.com/pg/paulaharmonwrites
https://www.goodreads.com/paula_harmon
https://twitter.com/Paula_S_Harmon

BOOKS BY LIZ HEDGECOCK

To check out any of my books, please visit my Amazon author page at http://author.to/LizH. If you follow me there, you'll be notified whenever I release a new book.

The Magical Bookshop (6 novels)
An eccentric owner, a hostile cat, and a bookshop with a mind of its own. Can Jemma turn around the second-worst secondhand bookshop in London? And can she learn its secrets?

Pippa Parker Mysteries (6 novels)
Meet Pippa Parker: mum, amateur sleuth, and resident of a quaint English village called Much Gadding. And then the murders began…

Caster & Fleet Mysteries (6 novels, with Paula Harmon)
There's a new detective duo in Victorian London … and they're women! Meet Katherine and Connie, two young women who become partners in crime. Solving it, that is!

Mrs Hudson & Sherlock Holmes (3 novels)
Mrs Hudson is Sherlock Holmes's elderly landlady. Or is she? Find out her real story here.

Maisie Frobisher Mysteries (4 novels)
When Maisie Frobisher, a bored young Victorian socialite, goes travelling in search of adventure, she finds more than she could ever have dreamt of. Mystery, intrigue and a touch of romance.

Sherlock & Jack (3 novellas)
Jack has been ducking and diving all her life. But when she meets the great detective Sherlock Holmes they form an unlikely partnership. And Jack discovers that she is more important than she ever realised…

Halloween Sherlock (3 novelettes)
Short dark tales of Sherlock Holmes and Dr Watson, perfect for a grim winter's night.

For children
A Christmas Carrot (with Zoe Harmon)
Perkins the Halloween Cat (with Lucy Shaw)
Rich Girl, Poor Girl (for 9-12 year olds)

BOOKS BY PAULA HARMON

THE MURDER BRITANNICA SERIES
Murder Mysteries set in 2nd Century Britain
mybook.to/MurderBritanniaSeries

THE MARGARET DEMERAY SERIES
Historical Mysteries set in the lead-up to World War 1
mybook.to/MargaretDemeraySeries

OTHER BOOKS BY PAULA HARMON
https://paulaharmon.com/books-by-paula-harmon/

SHORT STORIES BY PAULA HARMON & VAL PORTELLI
viewbook.at/PHWeirdandpeculiartales

AUDIOBOOKS BY PAULA HARMON
https://paulaharmon.com/audiobooks/

WHITE RHINO BOOKS

Printed in Great Britain
by Amazon